The Party's Over

The Party's Over

Four attempts to define a

love story

———

Juan Goytisolo

Translated from the Spanish by José Yglesias

GROVE PRESS, INC.
NEW YORK

To

Maurice-Edgar Coindreau

Originally published in Spain by
Seix Barral under the title *Fin
de fiesta*, copyright © 1962 by
Editorial Seix Barral, S.A.

Library of Congress Catalog Card Number: 66-27833

First Printing

Manufactured in the United States of America

First

THEY ARRIVED when the season was coming to an end. The sun was no longer as strong as in July; in the morning, a cool breeze blew, a warning of autumn's winds; and the days began to grow shorter. They got off the bus, loaded down with suitcases, duffle bags, wicker cases, and a mysterious object wrapped in canvas that the conductor clearly had a hard time setting down on the sidewalk. The young bucks and little boys out on the *Paseo* at that hour watched with curiosity. The package was about three feet high, and the canvas came to a kind of peak at the back. When he returned from the hotel, Damiana's husband, who had carried the package inside, said it was a sewing machine.

'A sewing machine? What for?'

Everybody in the village was asking the same question. We had seen many foreigners come with photographic equipment, portable radios, movie cameras, and even tape recorders, but who the devil would have thought of bringing a sewing machine on his vacation? Also, the fact that they had come by bus and not in their own car like the other clients of the hotel was cause for speculation. Tourists who travelled on the regular bus line always stayed at the inn. None of them that I could remember had gone on to stay at the hotel. While she served me lunch, Mother wanted to know what they looked like, what language they spoke. . . .

'I don't know,' I answered.

And, unfortunately, there was no way of knowing. The

hotel staff was much too proud of the gilt buttons on their uniforms to let us in on their talk. Witnesses of the happy life of the rich, they had no desire to share their secrets with anyone.

'What are they like?' sighed my mother. 'Young? Old?'

I told her the woman looked about thirty and the man in his twenties. Both were tall and blue-eyed, wore jeans and silk shirts and fishermen's sandals. That didn't satisfy Mother, and she quizzed me about their luggage. What were their suitcases like? How many? Someone had told her they had given Damiana's husband a good tip, and Mother's round eyes, with their watery irises, shone with excitement.

'I'm sure they must be refined people. If you got to be friends with them and they came to the house . . .'

That's the way Mother is. Since she was widowed, she spends all her time imagining events that will suddenly change our luck for the better. She was obsessed with the guests at the hotel, and every time a new guest arrived she made plans to invite him to dinner and then rent him a room at some fantastic price.

'They charge three hundred pesetas for room and board at the hotel. Maybe four hundred. I'd do the same for two hundred fifty, and they'd eat meat every day of the week. And French toast. And rice pudding with cinnamon, the way you like it. You ought to tell them, son. If they're looking for a restful place, it'd be cheaper for them.'

I was used to her daydreams, and they made no more impression on me than the sound of rain. Mother never bothered to follow them through. She was content with feeling rich for a few hours, with dreaming that she had crashed the circle of the hotel's privileged guests. She filled her life with movie magazines and radio serials, and had become removed from what was really happening around her.

As for me, that summer I thought only about Ramon. In the morning, while he went out with tourists who rented his boat and had a good time teaching foreign girls how to swim, I would take my textbooks to the beach and make believe I was reviewing my lessons under the hotel's beach umbrellas. Mother had enrolled me for the fall at a Catholic college in Granada, and, on the advice of the Fathers, I was supposed to be reviewing the manuals for the sixth course, so I would be at the same level as the other students. Instead, I spied on the bathers for hours on end. Once in a while, I would dive into the water and splash around for a few minutes like a fish. Time passed slowly, imperceptibly. The circular façade of the hotel shone like the quarterdeck of a great liner, the sea dashed against the rocks of the promontory, and heat waves blurred the view of the town in the distance. By the time I came to, it was time to eat.

On the other hand, I was free afternoons and evenings. Ramon would wait for me at the boat, or would be having a drink at one of the eating stands on the beach, and then I would help him mend his purse seine or bait the hooks on the gang lines. I've always preferred the beach on the other side of the cape to the town beach; the horizon is wider there, the sand thicker, and the thatched cane stands and boats make it livelier and more active. The hills in the distance merge into each other until they disappear from sight, the sky looks like an immense blue lake, and the cherimoya trees and cane fields beyond the coast road form a thick backdrop, cut in two by the chimney of the sugar refinery.

At dusk, when the last bathers went back to the hotel,

Ramon would rig the boat and make for the tip of the cape. He rowed beautifully, and with each stroke the beach became smaller, as if it were foreshortened. I liked to watch him as he dipped the oars in the water, his muscles tense with the effort. I thought I'd like to have a body like his when I grew up. Ramon had lived by the sea since he was a child and knew every inch of the coast-line. When he arrived at a fishing spot, he would take out the lines from the bow and let me handle the oars. That was the moment to cast the lines, then row slowly back-ward so that the lines wouldn't get snarled. When the sinkers touched bottom and the cork floats reappeared on the surface, Ramon would row back toward the cove, and we would spend the time talking and smoking one cigarette after another until it was time to draw in the lines.

On days when the sea was rough and we could not go out to the rocks to fish, Ramon would get a rake and we would go clamming along the shore. Every once in a while Mother asked why I came back so late, what was I doing all that time. There was no way of getting her to understand that at sea there's not a moment's boredom. There's always something to do – mending nets, bailing water, tracking a dragnet. I had told her a thousand times, hoping to convince her, but my explanations were always useless. Mother never listened and would sud-denly start talking about guests at the hotel: why didn't I get friendly with them instead of wasting my time with fishermen? 'Maybe there are some guests who are un-happy with the food and would gladly accept my offer; our luck could change.' Finally, tired of putting up with her fantasies, I would run out and look for Ramon at the café.

The men get together there after dinner, to drink a glass of red wine and play *rentoy*. Others hang around the sidewalk benches talking, or sit on the veranda dead drunk. There are many drunks in town, and you can hear them along the paths that climb up to the hills, shouting and singing until all hours. I would sit with the players at a table and listen to their conversations. They talked about the day's catch, the sea's moods, the next sugar cane harvest. Often they would comment on the women bathers' figures, and tease Ramon.

'If you need help,' they'd say to him, 'remember us. We're always ready to oblige.'

At the beginning of the summer a tall stringy German woman had almost drowned near the rocks and Ramon had brought her up unconscious and given her artificial respiration. To thank him, the woman had given him a watch. Since then, Ramon's friends pretended that he had taken advantage of her and labelled him a Don Juan.

'A-ah, didn't you have yourself a time that day!' sighed Damiana's husband.

'Imagine taking advantage of that stick!' exclaimed the guy they called Heredia. 'There was nothing there to enjoy. She slipped out of his hands like a fish . . . she was so flat up front. You could eat her on Friday and it wouldn't even be a sin.'

Ramon was the only one who said nothing. Actually, their talk bored him, and he preferred to chat with just me alone when we were out fishing. Once he confided that he had a girl friend in Motril, and although he said it casually, I was sure that they would end up getting married.

'What's your friend like?' I'd ask on days when he'd left town on his bicycle. I was a little jealous of his escapades, and Ramon would only smile broadly and muss up my hair with one hand.

That night the game of *rentoy* had hardly begun when

Heredia pointed toward the street and said, 'Look who's coming.'

We all turned to look. The foreigners who had arrived on the bus that morning were walking hand in hand under the palm trees, her head on his shoulder. They stopped for a moment to look at the moon rising above the cape like a round, illuminated balloon; then, making a right angle, they came straight to the café.

'The café!' Mother exclaimed when she learned this, her cheeks pink with excitement. 'Why go to the café?'

No one knew. Usually the hotel guests go dancing in the gardens around the pool after dinner and never dare to mix with us. But it hadn't been this, particularly, that had surprised us; it was the way they acted. When they entered the café, the woman had recognized Damiana's husband and smiled at him. The man ordered two cognacs. 'Tall ones,' he said. Taking advantage of their being so close, I looked them over. The woman had blond hair, regular features, and a certain arrogance in her eyes that made her very attractive. The man was red-haired and pale. He looked as if all his blood had gone up into his hair. While the card game lasted, they remained quiet, holding hands under the table. When they finished the cognac, they ordered another round. Though it was slow going, they spoke in Spanish. The fishermen looked at the woman's bare shoulders, but their stares did not seem to bother the couple. Once in a while the man smiled. Later, they paid the waiter and drifted away on the *Paseo*. Mother said that they were doubtless bored at the hotel.

The next day it was very hot. I went to the beach early in the morning, and there they were, stretched out in front of the umbrellas, their bodies smeared with oil.

The man wore trunks with a flower print, and the woman a two-piece suit that left her belly uncovered. Leaning on the railing of the *Paseo*, a group of fishermen stood looking down at them.

It was so hot that I couldn't keep my mind on anything. I tried several times to open the mathematics book, but each time I had to close it again, unable to keep up the effort. The haze dimmed the landscape, and I drowsily watched the waves breaking on the sand. Two fishing boats passed by on their way back from trawling. The horizon was a blurred blue line. The woman swam energetically toward the rocks, and when she got to one of the reefs, she waved in the direction of the beach. The man waved back. He had been sitting on a colored towel cutting the pages of a book, and he got up.

'Are there jellyfish?' he asked.

I said no, there weren't any. The man then showed me some scars on his instep. Three thin, dark, parallel stripes.

'Did that happen to you here?'

'Not here. In Italy.'

He walked to the shore and wet his hair with one hand. The woman kept on waving from the reef. She called to him to join her, but the man said no. The usual bunch of onlookers had dispersed little by little in search of other tourists, and I dived into the water. The owner of the eating stand had lent me his underwater equipment, and I headed out toward the cape. When I returned, the couple were gone from the beach.

The best times I had that summer were with Ramon when his friends came with him, and he and I joined them in fishing from shore. Fishing with a purse seine is much more exciting than trawling from a boat. I would stay on the beach taking care of the cast while he flung the net from the boat and turned round to drop the other end on shore. The catch is hauled from land, and as you pull it in, the lines begin to appear on top of the water, the nets get smaller, and the fish caught in the purse seine get excited and start to jump. The people at the eating stands would gather round to watch, and I enjoyed being in the midst of men pulling in unison, my body toasted by the sun and my face on fire with the effort. In the purse seine were jurels, flatfish, ox-eyed mackerel, horse mackerel, sardines. The women emptied the fish into boxes, and I would help the men to haul in the nets.

When, that same afternoon, I saw the foreigners among the crowd of onlookers, I felt flattered by their presence. I threw out my chest, tensed the muscles of my arms, and adopted an athletic stance. The woman still had her bathing suit on and was following our movements with interest. The man was wearing bright-colored shorts and a shirt. While we pulled in the line, they exchanged a few words with the owner of the eating stand. They wanted to know why the net was pulled from the land, and pointed vaguely toward the sea. Then they sat down among the boats and, when we had finished our job, the man lit a cigarette and hired Ramon's boat.

The setting sun softened the outline of the crest of the mountain and drowned the shore in a yellowish, languid light. The hills covered with almond trees were now gray, and here and there explosions of red earth spattered them with stains of color. Ramon had winked at me when he had started rowing, and I impatiently awaited his return. I passed the time looking at the cemetery, the white chimney of the sugar refinery, the thick foliage of the cherimoya trees. I thought of next winter in Granada when I'd be far from the sea and my friends, and suddenly I felt terribly depressed.

When the sun set, the hills looked like pasteboard, the sea lost its blue tones, and a flock of birds crossed the sky above the bay and alighted among the cane fields beyond the road. The boat returned a little later, and Ramon helped the couple jump ashore. The man stayed behind a moment to talk to us. The woman was trembling with cold, and ran to the hotel to dress.

'Where are they from?' I asked when they had left.

'Sweden. The man writes for a newspaper.'

The fishermen were listening too, and when we were alone Ramon told me that the couple had insulted each other in their own language during the whole trip, and at the cove the husband had gone off to climb the cliffs, leaving the two of them alone on the beach.

'How about her? What did she do?'

'Nothing,' he answered, laughing. 'She talked to me a little and then went swimming.'

There was an argument at the café that night. The owner of the beach stand maintained that men in other countries didn't know how to manage their women and then, well, what happens happens. 'A woman who shows her belly to men is a prostitute,' he said. The pharmacist answered that in Spain people had no freedom of action and lived as they had in the days of the Moors. 'In other countries,' he explained, 'women swim nude and nothing happens.' 'Because all the men are fairies,' answered the owner of the beach stand. 'I guarantee you, my wife doesn't show her belly to anyone.'

The others joined in and said that Andalusians were different and that if any women around there went swimming half-naked there'd be fighting with knives.

'Women belong at home with the children,' one of them concluded.

'That's what I was saying. We're still living in the days of the Moors,' the pharmacist said ironically.

After mass Sunday, Mother took me for a walk with her along the *Paseo* and, as usual, pointed to the hotel. She said Soraya was coming to Spain – she'd heard it on the radio the night before – and began to curse her bad luck and to lament how little I helped her. 'In places like the hotel you can't really rest. What a busy woman like her needs is rest. She'd be much better off at our house for half the price. I'm sure they charge her a fortune at the hotel, and she probably leaves half of what they serve on her plate. . . .'

She was so busy talking that she didn't even notice that the Swedish couple were coming down the stairs and waving at me. A few moments later, as if coming out of a dream, she recalled that they had waved and looked at me all confused. 'Do you know them?'

I told her who they were, and escaped before she got over her surprise. On Sundays the beach is completely different from what it is on other days. The fishermen do not go out, and the eating stands are filled with petit-bourgeois who come out by bus from Granada and kill time fishing with poles and lazing in the sun like lizards. Ramon had gone to Motril on his bicycle, and I drifted from one place to another without knowing what to do. In front of the hotel, I whiled away my time looking over the cars parked on the esplanade. Most were French from Morocco, there were a few German ones, and a Rolls with a Gibraltar license plate. A gypsy pulling a donkey was offering his water jug to the thirsty, and I spent twenty *centimos* for a swallow. I continued along the *Paseo*, and when I saw the couple, I retraced my steps and went down to lie on the beach.

'Lots of sun,' said the man with a smile.

'Yes.'

'In my country it doesn't get hot. Clouds and cold.'

The woman asked me about Ramon. I told her he was away.

'Are you a fisherman too?'

'No. A student.'

'What are you studying?'

I explained as best I could. The onlookers standing around didn't take their eyes off her, and I was proud of my boldness.

'I need two years to finish.'

'What will you do then?'

'I don't know yet.'

The woman took out a tube of lotion from her bag and spread it carefully on her thighs.

'My father came to Spain during the war.'

'As a soldier?'

'He loved Spain very much. He was a doctor.'

I said I didn't like medicine, and she readjusted her bathing suit strap, laughing, and ran to the water.

Beginning in September the sun goes down behind the hills, the cherimoyas ripen in the field, and the heat slackens. It's the best time of the summer. The sky is tinged with red just before sunset, the moon shines like a circus spotlight at night, and the sea is transparent and fresh and tastes like melon rind.

The houses of the summer residents were beginning to close, and on the esplanade of the hotel the line of cars was starting to thin out. Mother counted them every morning and returned overjoyed. 'Six. Six of them have left. At this rate the place will be empty in a week.' Every day she'd ask me about the Swedish couple and complain that I was no help to her.

I continued to go out with Ramon. The couple now regularly came to our beach, and the four of us would then go out in the boat. After dropping his gang lines, Ramon would row out to the cove, and we would swim beneath the cliffs or sunbathe until sundown. The husband often questioned us about the fishing. He wanted to know how much the men earned and if it was enough to live on. The woman would reach over her shoulder and untie the strap of her bathing suit and then read lying face down. She had a fine, very tanned body, and her rump was round and well shaped. From time to time she sat up, held the top of her suit up with her knees, and smoked, paying no attention to us.

One day we went out to the rocks for sea urchins. Ramon, in underwater equipment, would dive in and pass them on to me as he tore them off with a knife. When the basket was full, we returned to the cove and ate them with a little lemon juice. The husband had bought a bottle of wine in town, a dark red, thick wine, ripe with years, which left a slightly bitter taste in one's mouth. When we finished, we were all a little high. The woman proposed a swim to the point of the cape to Ramon, and he looked over at the husband before accepting. The husband said it was a fine idea, and the two of them ran to the shore and dived in the water.

The beach smoked in the heat. The sea was perfectly still and there was not a cloud in the sky. The man lay down by the boat and passed me a pack of Chesterfields. He asked if the people in town were interested in politics. I said no, and we spent a long time in silence, dulled by sleep and wine.

When they returned, Ramon looked changed. His eyes shone in a curious way and they kept coming back to the woman. She explained that she had had a marvellous swim, one of the very best she'd ever had. Then she added a few words in Swedish.

The husband looked at Ramon with arched eyebrows. He too had noticed the change and smiled with amusement. 'How about you?' he said to Ramon, 'did you enjoy yourself?'

'Very much.'

'Marvellous. Love, sun, wine . . . the kid and I slept for a while.'

That same night I asked Ramon what he had done with the woman, and instead of winking as he had done the first day he said dryly, 'Nothing.' We were sitting at the café, and he had the abashed, tense expression of a boy who's come home on tiptoes after an adventure he must keep to himself. Once in a while he would squint and watch the shadows on the *Paseo* closely. Finally, when it was evident they were not coming, he seemed to relax a little and went off to play *rentoy* with his friends.

For a while the Swedish couple made themselves scarce. Ramon waited in vain with the boat every day, and at the last minute he would take me fishing at the cove. Although we had not discussed it again, I knew he was thinking about her. In the café, he played distractedly at *rentoy*, and his eyes shone like a cat's each time someone entered.

One night Damiana's husband said that, according to the hotel employees, the Swedish couple spent their time arguing, and then would lock themselves up in their room and drink until they were dead drunk.

'If you ask me, I think they've got bats in their belfry,' he added. 'Since when does a man pass the time embroidering handkerchiefs?'

'Embroidering handkerchiefs ?'

'That's what I said. The sewing machine belongs to him. Maybe in their country guys wear skirts instead of pants.'

I was overjoyed now that I was alone again with Ramon, and I thought the couple had forgotten us. In three weeks my vacation would be over and I wanted to enjoy my last few days of freedom. I had given up studying. My mother's lamentations bored me, and I went down to the beach to help the fishermen draw in the nets. Soon the hotel would close down. Its last guests were sunbathing on the terrace, and I told myself that sooner or later the Swedes were bound to leave.

On the day of the September Virgin, the couple had a visitor. On the esplanade was a dusty car with an S above the spare tyre. Its owner, a blond man, had a pirate's mustache and acted as if he were a close friend of theirs. At midday the three of them went swimming out at the rocks. The new arrival brought underwater equipment and killed several fish with a gun. There was dancing that afternoon, and soon after it started, he showed up again with them and danced with the wife, holding her very close, while the husband drank cognac after cognac at the bar. By dinner time he was blind drunk, and his wife and the other man plunked him down in the hotel lobby and went walking hand in hand until they disappeared on the outskirts of town. The next morning the intruder's car was gone. Ramon and I spent a long time on the beach, but the Swedish couple didn't leave their room.

Two days later, when no one was expecting them any longer, they turned up at the café. I noticed immediately because Ramon suddenly started trembling, and I turned and waved at them. The woman wore a décolleté blouse which set off her tan; the man was as pale as always, and his hair looked so red it was like tow.

They had ordered cognac with a little ice. The woman looked nervous and downed hers almost in one gulp. The bartender came back immediately with the bottle. For a while they smoked without exchanging a word. The woman kept breaking the toothpicks in half and throwing them on the floor. Then she started talking in a flat monotone, as if she had turned on a record. The husband listened to her without any apparent emotion. He too emptied his glass and asked for another. The woman had finished the toothpicks on their table, and she spoke louder and louder now, her voice high-pitched and vibrant. Once or twice she stopped, perhaps waiting for an answer, but the man said nothing. His eyes were obstinately fixed on some point in the shadows of the *Paseo*. Then the woman grabbed him by the collar of his shirt and spat out a word of two syllables, five, ten, fifteen times, just as if she were driving in a nail. Her hands were rigid and her lips trembled. For a moment I thought she was going to slap him, but she changed her mind and slipped out into the dark as suddenly as she had arrived.

Slowly the fishermen went back to playing *rentoy*. No one had ever seen anything like it at the café, and the man's behaviour had seemed even more scandalous than hers: why did he allow himself to be insulted publicly? Didn't he have any red blood in his veins? For much less than that, men in my country take out their knives and get even. Everyone can remember some exemplary punishment: wives whose hair was shaved off, an ear mutilated, a nose cut. 'In Motril when I was a boy . . .' you'd hear, or 'One day in Salobreña . . .' The Swede, however, was sitting there very quietly and smiling as if

nothing had happened. My friends looked at him scorn-
fully, and I felt like yelling at him to go out and find the
woman and teach her a lesson.

He didn't do it, and the next day he showed up on
the beach with her. The old men mending the nets
stopped their work and looked at them as they came toward us. The man was wearing shorts and a print shirt;
she had on a bathing suit and a blue rubber bathing cap.
They stopped in front of Ramon's boat.

'Are you free?'

Ramon nodded, and we shoved off without a word.
The eating stands were empty, and an autumn sun outlined the naked scar of the cliffs and the faded, quiet
hills. Among the almond trees the red earth looked
flushed with rouge. Ramon rowed briskly, happy to be
using up his energy on something. With each stroke his
muscles hardened and his Adam's apple rose like a piston.
The man watched him intently during the whole trip.
The woman sat in the middle of the boat and looked only
at the water.

When we arrived at the cove, we beached the boat. A
band of seagulls rose up like a vortex of feathers and
flew toward the lighthouse, tracing spirals. The sea
looked bluer than ever, and you could see down through
it to the rippled sand at the bottom and to the stones
covered with sea urchins and anemones. The woman invited Ramon to swim out to the rocks. Ramon accepted
without even looking at the husband. I didn't know what
to do with myself, and my cheeks burned with shame.
If they were going to repeat the idyll of the first day, why
didn't they find some other place? The husband was no
doubt used to it, but why rub it in?

I couldn't help pitying the man's smile, and I decided to
climb the cliffs. As I climbed, the blue horizon widened,

and I couldn't help thinking about next winter in Granada and feeling sad. Adios get-togethers at the café and boat trips; good-bye fishing, swimming, beach, excursions, and friends. Adios. When you're far from the sea, every season is the same. It doesn't matter whether the sun shines or it rains or it's cloudy. Time stops meaning anything. Life is like sleepwalking.

When I came down, the man was lying face down, sunbathing. During my absence, he had taken off his shirt and rolled it into a pillow. His body was not hard and knotty like Ramon's. It was thin and fragile, and his shoulder blades stuck out like prickly pear leaves. He smiled and asked me where I had gone. I told him. Later, he passed me his pack of cigarettes and asked if I had a girl friend. I shook my head.

'And your friend? Does he have one?'

'I don't know.'

Neither the woman nor Ramon gave any sign of returning, and we talked about them as if they had not left us. The man assured me that he found Ramon very nice, and I was on the point of saying, 'Do you say that because he gets along well with your wife?' but his ingenuousness and the helpless expression in his eyes disarmed me.

'It's true he's nice, but not with everyone.'

The Swede let sand run through his fingers, and he looked at me perplexed. 'In this life you can't please everybody,' he said.

Little woolly clouds moved across the sky of the bay, and he lay down on the sand again and closed his eyes. The woman and Ramon had now rounded the headlands of the point and were approaching slowly, scarcely disturbing the water. Their heads floated in the sea like two heads of walking canes. The woman was swimming ahead wearing her blue cap, with Ramon a few yards to the left, tanned and uncombed. While she was walking out of the water toward us, he stood for a few moments on the shore, shaking himself like a bulldog.

The boat was still beached on the sand and, as the wind freshened, waves dashed against its keel. The woman laughed and said she was sorry they were so late. As she sat down she took off her cap, and against her smooth, tanned skin her hair looked blonder than ever. Ramon said nothing, as if he were immersed in an inexplicable inner happiness. The husband continued to lie face down on the sand, and we talked about the heat and the beach. I had been afraid of a scene like last night's at the café and breathed a sigh of relief. The man went on smiling, as if what was happening between the two of them didn't matter to him at all. After a moment, he took out a cigar case and offered it to Ramon.

'Would you like one?'

Ramon looked at him for a few seconds, puzzled, and shook his head. 'No, thanks.'

'Don't you like them?' The man looked at him in turn in surprise.

'Yes, I like them all right. But I don't feel like one now.'

'Go on, take one. It would please me if you tried this too.'

Ramon blushed slightly. 'I wouldn't want to offend you . . .' he began.

'I *would* be offended.'

'Well, then, I'll smoke it.' He grabbed the cigar. 'No, I have a light, thanks.'

And that was all. At lunch time, Ramon took the oars, and we returned to the beach. The man paid him for the rental of the boat and went off arm in arm with the woman.

I was beginning to tire of the whole thing and asked Ramon if he had also been paid for the excursion to the rocks. I thought Ramon would laugh, but he said nothing and looked irritated.

'That's his wife, and you have a fiancée,' I said.

'Well, go and find a woman for yourself,' he answered, exasperated.

I went home without saying good-bye. The woman had come between us and I hated her with all my heart. That same afternoon I went to visit a girl who worked in a beauty parlor in Granada. She was a friend of Mother's and was spending a short vacation in town. I took her to the movies. Last summer we had gone walking in the sugar cane fields, and I knew that she would not act like a prude the way the other girls did. I got what I wanted without much effort, and after dinner I went to pick her up at the inn and persuaded her to accompany me to the café. My friends were playing *rentoy* as usual, but even though we spent more than an hour there chitchatting, Ramon didn't show up.

I started swimming at the town beach again. I expected that Ramon would think better of what he'd said to me, and worrying about where I was, would come to look for me. But the first day went by slowly, boringly, and Ramon didn't show up at the café or the beach. I waited a couple of days more, feeling somewhat disappointed, and the way the place looked remained the same: its cane huts deserted, the young men clam-digging with rakes, and the lazy old men sunning themselves. Ramon seemed to have vanished. At the café, I heard that he went out in his boat with the Swedes, and once when the husband crossed the street in front of us, Heredia smiled like a brute and said, 'Oh, if Manolete takes him on, what a killing there's going to be, man!'

I spent the day walking about from one place to the other, but I would not give in. At home, Mother read about the American ambassador's scheduled trip through Andalusia and dreamed of putting him up. Her lamentations would get on my nerves, and when I was sure I wouldn't run across anybody I would go to the beach and help the men haul in their nets.

These were days of intense sadness. All the foreigners had left the hotel, and the eating stands had closed. The owner of the place we usually went to dismantled his stand one morning, while the old men were dyeing the nets on the sand. Everything announced that autumn was almost here. The hills paled as the green of the almond trees became faint; farther off in the distance the sun lit up the mountain theatrically. Soon they would start to harvest the grapes.

At night, I ambled along the steep paths up the hill, and after touring all the bars I climbed the rocks on the cape and stared at the windows of the hotel. I could see the waiters in their white jackets and the showy frescoes on the walls, but only once did I hit on what I was looking for. The Swedish couple were seated in the middle of the empty dining room, both their heads in profile: a red one that looked dishevelled; the other brown and yellow. They were drinking a dark liqueur, rolling it around their tongues, and the woman was stroking the man's hand. A waitress pulled the curtains, and I didn't get to see them again.

I had begun to regret my stupid quarrel with Ramon. It was more than a week since we had talked, and I knew nothing about him, except what I heard from his friends. That is how I learned that he had not gone to Motril on

Sunday and had hung around the beach waiting for the woman. Damiana's husband had seen him after supper, still lurking around the hotel like a wolf. That night the Swedish couple did not leave their room.

Two days later as I was getting up – I had gone to the movies the night before with the beauty parlor operator, and it was almost eleven in the morning – Mother came into my room and said, 'Do you know what's happened?' Her hair was mussed and her lips were trembling with emotion. 'Your friend, the redhead, almost left this world. They came for him in an ambulance this morning. It seems he's already out of danger, thank God.' And instead of answering my questions, she began to complain that it was my fault for letting them stay at the hotel and not bringing them to our house. 'I knew it would end badly,' she said. 'I knew it. Poor man, who wouldn't go crazy in a place like that.' I didn't wait for her to finish and ran to the *Paseo*. My heart was thumping. In front of the hotel there were half a dozen curiosity seekers, and for once the bellhop forgot the dignity of his uniform and talked and talked. 'Jesus, what a bender. They didn't leave their room for two days. The waitress kept taking wine up to them. Not the ordinary kind either, I can tell you. Expensive stuff with a good label. When I went to take the bags down this morning, I swear there were at least fifteen bottles. The sommelier – and he's a guy who's been around a lot – told me: "I've seen some crazy guests in my day, but none like this couple." And he's got more good sense than a saint. Imagine her, cheating on him with every man that comes along, and him acting as if nothing were happening.' Then, as some more people came up to listen, he repeated for their benefit that the man had taken a whole bottle of sleeping pills, thinking they were aspirin. When she woke up, the woman found him unconscious, but managed to revive him with a little ammonia. By the time the ambulance arrived, he had vomited several times and was able to walk out on his own two feet. 'Take my word for it, he looked like a corpse. The chambermaid on their floor is very sensitive, and she almost had a fit when she saw him. And the others too, don't let them tell you any different. You can take it from me, I don't know how I stand it.'

The children were running around the beach naked, and looked around at the closed, empty eating stands. Ramon was sitting next to his boat in swimming trunks and a faded blue undershirt. He hadn't shaved in several days, and his eyes were puffy from lack of sleep. When he saw me, he tried to smile.

I helped him push the boat into the water, and we rowed slowly toward the cape. The moon was still perched high in the sky, like a cuttlefish bone, and sky and sea joined at the horizon in a blurred gray line. I looked at the cypresses in the cemetery, the hotel, the hills beyond, and I understood suddenly that my vacation was over and Ramon and the boat and what had happened with the Swedish couple were things of the past: they were stories of the summer that I would remember in school later on, when I would be far from the sea and friendless.

The sand on the cove gleamed in the sunlight and we threw ourselves down on the beach. The seagulls were white spots against the rocky promontory, behind which Ramon some days ago had disappeared with the woman. Now my friend smoked in silence, and I found him sad and older looking.

'It was nothing, you know,' he said simply. 'I'm going to Motril next Sunday.'

Second

FROM THE VERY BEGINNING I had followed what happened to the man with interest. Every morning I bought the newspaper only to find out about him, and I savored his triumphs against the old oppressors as something intimate and personal. In my office, I had half a dozen photos from an old issue of *Life* in which the other actors in the drama also appeared. His story had not yet become a tragedy; the man escaped dangers and eluded ambushes as skilfully as a tightrope walker. His was the face of an intelligent, good devil, a face that perfectly matched his genius as circus magician and trapeze artist. With enemies and traitors on all sides, he advanced fearlessly along the tightrope. Often, when he seemed about to fall – and like any merciful, sensitive spectator I was ready to close my eyes – some last-minute, unexpected pirouette would manage to straighten him out and hold him miraculously in balance. One day – for no reason at all – luck abruptly abandoned him. All of us who loved him knew this had happened, and we began to fear for him. In the news photographs, from September on he seemed careworn and absorbed in thought, as if he were already conjecturing what meaning his destiny held. Little by little, the spiderweb had closed in on him; newspapers published the smiling faces of his enemies. Their playing the role of good guys prevented them, however, from staining their own hands with his blood, and they had decided to turn him over to the executioner for thirty pieces of silver. Later, the news agencies distributed pictures of him beaten and fallen.

In one of the pictures he was shown handcuffed, an object of compassionate curiosity for those whose children some day would be free men thanks to him. The expression on his face became engraved in my mind and was not erased for a second during the hours that followed the announcement of his disappearance and the brutal notice of his death. I had gone down with Ana for a walk, and in the street Rafael showed us the newspaper headlines. 'I've decided to shed my skin,' he said. 'The color white disgusts me.'

That was in February, and four months had passed since then. Nevertheless, when I saw the crowd of curious onlookers and stopped the car, I had the feeling that I was reliving a familiar experience, and realized that the picture of the handcuffed man was still fresh in my memory. The man the sightseers had surrounded on the road to the free port was still young, about thirty or thirty-five; he was tied to the grating of a window, with his back to the crowd and his forehead leaning on one of the iron bars. The group was watching him with respect and quietly discussing how he had been captured. Someone said that he had stolen flour from a warehouse.

In a few moments a police jeep arrived, and the spectators opened a way for the policemen. The man shackled to the window turned to look at them slowly. His face was covered with sweat. He was wearing a very worn jacket, no shirt; between the jacket's lapels you could see his ruddy chest, hairy up to his adam's apple; his toes peeked through the tip of his fiber sandals. I elbowed my way through to him and asked if I could help him.

'I'm a lawyer,' I added, raising my voice so that the police could hear me.

The man looked at me a few seconds; he had blue eyes, heavily shaded by thick eyelashes, and he shook his head. 'Thank you very much,' he said. 'I don't need any-thing.'

When they took him away in the jeep, the spectators dispersed. I examined the iron bars on the window once more before going back to my car. Loles was waiting for me, nervously biting her nails.

'What did he do?' she asked. 'Why did they take him away?'

'He's a dope.'

'A what?' She tilted her head and looked at me with her black, burning eyes.

'A thief,' I explained. 'Just a poor bastard.'

I drove under an arch of plane trees. Men on their way home from work were walking about in overalls and shirt-sleeves. After a hundred yards or so, I braked to let a truck go by.

'Alvaro.'

'Yes.'

I turned to look at her. Loles pulled me to her and kissed me with unhurried greediness.

'You're marvellous, do you know that?'

'No.'

'You're marvellous, I tell you. You pretend you have nothing on your mind, but I know that right now you're thinking about that man and how you could give him a hand. And what's more I'm sure you'll manage it. . . .'

'You're wrong. He didn't want a thing from me.'

'But you'll help him. I bet anything that you'll get him out of jail immediately.'

We kissed again. The driver of the Leyland behind us sounded his horn impatiently.

'Where are we going?' she said. 'I want to know all the places you know. That way, when I'm alone, I can come back to them, and it'll be as if I were with you.'

'It's seven. I promised to phone Ana.'

'Please, let me be with you a while.' Loles spoke entreatingly, and I looked at her checked blouse for a few moments, her short hair, her quick small hands.

'You're a child. Do you know what people are going to think when they see us together? That I'm a lecherous old man who spends his time following girls home from school.'

'They'll think that you're an intelligent, handsome man and that I'm lucky as hell to be with you.'

When we got to the turn, I headed for the esplanade where the trolleys turn around. I parked the car along the sidewalk and got out to look at the cemetery.

'Do you know this place?'

'No,' she answered. ' I don't know anything. Only what you've taught me.'

'My parents are buried here and my parents' parents. . . . Some day I'll show you the mausoleum.'

'Why not now?'

'It's late and they're probably closed. Come on, we'll go sit in the bar.'

The name of the place was written on a rectangular Coca-Cola sign. There were about a dozen tables on the sidewalk, and the awning was decorated with little colored flags.

The Andalusians who lived in the neighborhood were playing cards and clapping for service. A loudspeaker was broadcasting one of Farina's songs.

Loles sat down at the only free table, and I went up to the bar to ask for two cuba libres with gin. Inside there were some kids and some old men watching television. At the bar was a drunk with his shirt open. His shirt-tail peeked through his fly, and he was clumsily trying to hitch up his pants. The girl behind the counter smiled at me.

'A man asked for you yesterday,' she said.

'Do you know who it was?'

'A dark man with a scar. . . . Hey you!' She turned to one of the clients. 'What's the name of Juaneles' friend?'

'Which one? El Pepico?'

'No, the big guy with the scar.'

'Oh, I know. The one they call Zurguena. Were you looking for him?'

'I think he was looking for me.'

'I just saw him in front of his house about half an hour ago. Do you have his address?'

'No.'

'If you like, I'll show you the way. He lives back that way.'

'Forget it!' the girl protested. 'He'll come back. A bad penny always does. Don't you see the gentleman isn't alone?'

Loles was staring at the mountain. The Andalusians looked her up and down, and I waited for the girl to prepare the cuba libres. Rafael and I had discussed the cinematic possibilities of the place many times, and from the same spot where she was seated we had thought up projects for the future. The panorama of the cemetery was really unusual. At the peak the vaults glistened in the sun like blocks of enigmatic, modern apartments. Below, the huts scaled the slope and crept up toward the marble mausoleums and the funereal cypresses. An ambiguous frontier separated the world of the dead from that of the living. The whole thing looked so harmonious it was almost frightening.

I told Loles our idea for a film and added that we would never go through with our plan. 'We spend our lives talking about impossible things. One day, we'll die drunk with words.'

'I'm sure that if you plan to do something you do it,' she said.

'I thought so too when I was twenty. I was sure that one day I'd do something. I didn't know what, but something that would be new and useful at the same time. Now I'm over thirty and know that if I've done nothing until now, there's no reason to believe I'll do it in the future. Every day I feel more tired, older. . . .'

'That's not true,' Loles said. 'You're young and you do *thousands* of things. You're the best lawyer in the world. People listen to you in court and admire you. You have . . .' She spoke hurriedly as if afraid of being interrupted. 'You've got that gift of being interested in others, of winning their sympathy immediately. Why, when you enter a place, everyone looks at you. You're . . . you're . . .'

'Please, don't talk nonsense.'

'It's *not* nonsense.' Loles' cheeks were burning, and she kept twisting her hands feverishly. 'You're a real person, and you're serious about things. I can't stand your belittling yourself.'

We said no more for a moment, and I felt the weight of her glance, obstinate and stubborn, like a little girl's.

'I'm tired,' I said. 'When I'm on vacation, I'll feel better.'

'Where are you going?'

'I want to tour the south. Rafael went last year and was crazy about it. If nothing happens, I'll leave in a couple of weeks.'

'I'll go with you.'

'I'm not going alone. Ana is coming too.'

'It's all the same to me. I'll go with both of you.' She

said it in a defiant tone, and then her face became still, as if her mind had for a moment suspended all activity, waiting for my answer.

'You're very nice, but neither Ana nor I need company.'

'I won't bother you. I'll follow you wherever you go without grumbling and I'll do whatever you say.'

'Be reasonable,' I said. 'Since when do girls of your age travel with married men?'

'Since right now.' Her eyes shone as if she were about to cry. 'If it's not done, I'll be the first to do it.'

'Listen to me. Ana is my wife and she wants to be alone with me.'

'Everybody wants to be alone with you. I don't have to be your wife to want that.' Her childish anger seemed sincere. 'How long do you expect to be away?'

'A month . . . a month and a half. . . .'

'A month and a half without you,' she sighed.

'That's not long. You'll see. When your parents take you to the Pyrenees you'll forget about us.'

'That's not true. I won't forget you and I won't go with my parents. I'll stay in Barcelona, and I'll spend the day in places you've shown me. Right here, on this terrace.'

'You'll have a very good time.'

'I'll bring a notebook and write you. That way I'll at least be with you.'

There was a moment of silence. A woman was crossing the plaza pushing a small flower cart, and the last visitors in mourning were waiting at the trolley stop. It was still sunny at the top of the mountain.

'You're hateful,' Loles said. 'You know I'm dying to go with you, and you're only thinking of pleasing your wife.'

'You can't please everybody.'

'If you loved me a little, you'd try.'

'People like me always feel at fault. We'd like to be doing a million things at the same time, and when we do one we drop the rest.'

'Things?' she said. 'What kind of things?'

'I don't know. . . . Be an intellectual and also a man of action, a good father, a good lover, a good friend. . . . I can't be all these things at once, so my conscience is never at peace.'

'For me it would be enough if you were at peace with me.'

'Don't be a child. I've already told you it's impossible.'

'It's not for Ana.'

'You're wrong. Today, for example, I told her I'd telephone her.'

'She's got you every day. If I lived with you I could be generous too.'

'Ana is always generous.'

'I know that,' Loles said. 'Pay no attention to me. I talk just to hear the sound of my own voice.'

I got up with my empty glass and ordered a second round of cuba libres from the girl at the bar. An Andalusian had started singing soleares. Loles turned to look at him and immediately looked at me again.

'What cities do you plan to visit?' The sun had just set, and her face grew dark. 'I'm going to buy a guidebook and read it while you're travelling.'

'Don't be absurd.'

'I'm not absurd. I'm being practical. I want to be well organized while you're away.'

'It's no use, neither Ana nor I know where we'll go.'

'You don't?'

'We'll follow our noses. If we like a place, we'll stop and look around.'

'Never mind,' she said. 'I'll imagine the whole thing, and that will be better still.'

I drank a third cuba libre. When we got back to the car, we kissed slowly. Loles' mouth was warm, and she closed her eyes.

Ana had grown tired of waiting. I found a note from her on my desk and also a list of the phone calls that had come in that afternoon. Before going to meet her at the place she had told me to meet her, I looked up the number of the reporter on *El Caso* and asked him for news of the man who had been arrested. 'They caught him stealing flour on the road to the free port. I don't think he's at the prefecture yet.'

'I'll ask at the neighborhood police station. Do you know his name?'

'No.'

'Well, it doesn't matter.'

'When will you know something?'

'Call me tomorrow. I'm more likely to then.'

The address Ana had left turned out to be a little intimate theater, and the usher took us to our seats just as the curtain went up. Ana was in the first row with Rafael, Montse, the Ferrers, and Paco Iruña. When she saw us, she waved furtively.

The play was an original work by a friend of Tere's. It was an earthy drama, set in a Greek island, filled with men tormented by brutal passions and silent mothers in mourning. The protagonist made love to his sister in the wheat fields and then wiped away his sweat with a handkerchief and chanted in a lugubrious voice, 'It's the sun, it's the sun.' At the end, the invited audience applauded, and Loles and I fled laughing to the exit.

Ana came up the aisle on Paco Iruña's arm, wearing a gold and black blouse. Her dark tan made her look beautiful, and I thought I'd never seen her so pretty.

'Forgive me for standing you up,' said Loles. She'd hurried to kiss Ana and put her arm around her. 'It's all my fault. I'm in love with you and Alvaro. I can't live without you.'

'Where did you go?' Ana caught her chin and looked her straight in the face.

'Alvaro showed me the cemetery and the beach at the free port. He told me that when you were sweethearts you used to spend your afternoons there.'

'I suspected as much,' Ana said, laughing. 'Every time he wants to seduce someone he takes her to Casa Valero or to Montjuich. I bet he introduced you to one of his poor.'

'Today I only found a flour thief,' I joked. 'How about you? What have you been doing?'

'Since you weren't around, I took on the job of consoling her,' Iruña said.

'Whose idea was it to come here?'

'Tere's responsible,' Rafael said. 'She forced us.'

'What a liar he is. The author's my friend and I couldn't be rude to him. I warned you the play was bad.'

'What about supper?' I said.

There was a conference to decide where we'd go. Montse was talking about some dive on Gracia where they knew how to prepare steaks. Ana said she preferred the eating places along the Barceloneta. 'At least we'd be out in the open air. What do you think?'

She got into the car with Rafael, Loles, and Paco Iruña, and I drove down Vía Layetana toward the port. Ana said Rafael and Montse had had a quarrel about Ricardo Ferrer's wife. Rafael had insisted that Tere was a petit-bourgeois.

'Poor Ricardo wears himself out working, and Tere has made him move into a three thousand peseta flat and hired a maid to take care of the children.'

'Better leave them alone,' I said. 'I suppose they know what they're doing.'

'If Tere doesn't want to move out of the place, she could at least let the girl go. Otherwise, Ricardo will get into debt and start asking everyone for loans.'

'He's losing all his friends,' said Ana. 'No one asks him out because they don't want to put up with her.'

'Besides, she's jealous as hell. Do you know that she keeps track of every minute after he leaves the office? If he's just a little late, she goes down to the street to wait.'

'I'd love to know what she does the whole damned day.'

'She must spend it cultivating her intelligence,' said Loles.

'She's completely illiterate. As soon as you talk to her, there's no hiding the fact.'

'I don't understand why Ricardo puts up with her.'

'Just living with her is making him insensitive too. If he doesn't break away he'll turn into a moron.'

This is all we had talked about for months now, and I remembered the days when we believed in things and tried to help each other instead of destroying things and criticizing our friends' wives. The paralysis of doing nothing had caught up with us little by little, and the farther we strayed from reality the more helplessly we drowned in a tangle of psychological interpretations and conjectures.

There were no free parking spaces in front of the restaurant, so I parked in one of the alleys. As she got out of the car, Loles impulsively kissed Ana. Rafael kept on blathering about Ricardo's wife, and we all waited for Montse to arrive in their little bug.

The employees in the eating places kept signalling to us to come in. They looked like pimps – uniformed and obsequious – and Ricardo, when he arrived, recalled the heroic old days of the houses of prostitution. Finally we went into one of the restaurants, and the waiter sat us at a table by the beach. The moon was out, and you could see a few couples seated on the shore. When they brought the wine list, I ordered two bottles of Cariñena claret.

'Start cooling them right away,' I said.

I had a vial of Alka-Seltzer with me, and I got up for a glass of water. While the tablets dissolved, Ana went to the washroom, and I ran in after her and kissed her on the lips. She pushed me away brusquely.

'Let me go,' she said. 'Have you been drinking?'

'A couple of cuba libres, just to tone myself up.'

'You stink of gin like the other day. If you want to get drunk, please do it when I'm not around. It horrifies me to see you drunk.'

She started to comb her hair with quick, nervous motions and I watched her in the mirror, her image eroded by the light from the naked bulb.

'Besides, drinking is a nasty habit. No matter how much in love they may be, girls hate it.'

'I don't see what you mean by that.'

'Nothing,' she answered. 'You know as well as I do.'

She walked off without saying another word, and I went back to the bar and drank the glass of water and Alka-Seltzer. They had kept a place for me at the table between Loles and Tere. When I got back Rafael was having a lively discussion with Montse.

'You men are a vanishing race. The future is ours.'

'There are no impotent men. There *are* incompetent women.'

'What do you call competence?'

'Ask Alvaro. It's only right that he tell you.'

There was a chorus of laughter, and Ana said that that must have been in the faraway days of my youth. 'Now he prefers sentimental idylls. Time has made him lazy.'

'Pay some attention to your wife,' said Paco Iruña. 'If I were you I'd try never to be very far away from her.'

'No?' I said. 'Why?'

'Don't give him the wrong impression, for God's sake,' protested Ana. 'All I'd need would be for him to be jealous. That's one fault I won't put up with.'

'What faults *do* you put up with?' Loles asked.

'None really. People like Alvaro are used to being adored by others, and they've all got a natural propensity for taking themselves seriously. If I don't shake him up once in a while, he'd end up as conceited as a movie actor right, darling?'

The waiter brought a tray of appetizers and uncorked a bottle of Cariñena. The claret tasted good, and although there had not been time to cool it properly, it went down easily. While I poured, I told them the story of the flour thief, without too many details.

'Don't you know who he is?' asked Tere.

'Alvaro asked him if he wanted help but he said no.'

'Alvaro is out of touch with most things, but not when it comes to redeeming Humanity,' Ana announced.

Loles blushed and said, 'Does that seem so little?'

Ana exchanged a look with me. Then she suddenly broke into a laugh. 'No,' she said. 'If he were different, I probably wouldn't love him.'

She took hold of my hand affectionately and explained that I was annoyed with her because she had called me a drunk. 'I've given him a lecture on how vice enslaves and how alcoholism is passed on through the genes. . . . I love arguing, even when I know I'm wrong. I adore scenes.'

'You'd be happy with Rafael,' sighed Montse.

'Ricardo and I have a perfect understanding,' said Tere. 'We've been married three years and never have had a quarrel.'

'The dumb don't quarrel either,' Rafael murmured.

Ricardo watched us with a worried look, and Paco Iruña joined in. He said that often we men don't give women the support we owe them and ended with his usual plea for peace and harmony. He had the powerful neck of an oarsman or a fighter, and enormous, square, coarse hands. Ana approved with a nod.

'Let's talk of something else,' she said.

Her proposition found no adherents, and Rafael and Montse kept the argument going. Tere hung on to Ricardo as if she were afraid someone were going to tear him away any minute. Ana let Loles wear her earrings, and they kissed each other on the cheek. The Cariñena went quickly, and I ordered two more bottles.

'May I ask what you're thinking?' whispered Ana. 'You look furious with the whole world.'

She looked me up and down, and I lowered my voice and said I was tired.

'Then go home and sleep, but don't sit around here with that long face. I tell you it looks pitiful.'

'I'd like to get away, Ana. I'd like to get in the car and disappear for a couple of months. . . .'

'Meanwhile, do make an effort, please. Everyone's getting the impression that you drink just to put up with us.'

'Well, it's the simple truth,' I said.

A salvo of exclamations greeted the end of an anecdote by Montse. Loles must have heard our conversation because her hand searched me out under the table. I did make an effort and told a sick story about two gypsies during a famine. When I finished, everyone was choking with laughter, and I found I was worn out, my mind completely empty.

'Come on, tell another one,' said Tere.

'I'm out of training,' I answered. 'I don't go out much, so I'm not in shape.'

'Your wife is right,' exclaimed Iruña. 'Have you noticed? He's finished the Cariñena all by himself.'

'Rafael was drinking too,' Loles said accusingly.

'Let's get organized,' said Montse. 'Does anyone know a bar where we can get any marijuana?'

Iruña was scandalized, and we finally decided to take a turn around the neighborhood. On our way out, Loles took Ana's arm. Tere walked with Ricardo and Iruña. Rafael fell behind and paired off with me.

'What's troubling you?' he asked after a few seconds.

'I don't know,' I answered. 'I have the peculiar feeling that we're all dissolving – you, me, my wife. . . .' Rafael slowed his pace and stopped in front of me. 'We keep expecting the impossible and it's making us neurotic. If this goes on much longer, they'll have to lock us up.'

'What should we do? Take to the woods?'

'No, no, I'm not saying that.' My head ached, and I lit another cigarette. 'Not one of us can stand himself nor anyone else, for that matter. Once we used to talk about creating things. Now we're merciless about destroying everything.'

The others were waiting at the corner bar, and we reached them in silence. Inside, most of the clients were sitting with their backs to the street, attentively watching a television program. Montse ordered a round of cuba libres with gin. Ana had made a place for herself and Paco at the end of the bar and ostentatiously avoided looking at me.

'Whose idea was it to come here?' I said. 'The place looks sinister.'

No one answered, and suddenly Rafael began clowning and imitating Tere's voice: 'My man and I are one being and we love each other madly. . . . Oooh, ooh, pul-lease don't steal him from me!' Ricardo, taken aback, said nothing, and Montse intervened to remind us that we were out to enjoy ourselves, not to argue or fight.

'Hold your tongue, you hear?' Montse tried to stop him. 'You're drunk.'

'If you've trapped a hubby, take care of him, watch him like the apple of your eye. . . . Don't ever let him out of your sight!'

'Shut up.'

'Don't sleep. . . . A second's distraction can bring about the death of the artist.'

As he mimicked Tere, Rafael's face became paler and paler, and he walked off groggily to the men's room. Montse and Paco ran after him. The television program had ended, and on the screen there was a deployment of tanks and flags. One after the other the chiefs of the Movement came forward, getting larger on the screen and ending with the serene and grave close-up of the Caudillo, while emblems of Victory rippled in the background, and the sound track played the National Anthem. One by one the customers in the bar got up from their seats.

'Come on,' said Ana. 'Pay and let's go.'

Once in the street, Tere burst into tears and pulled at my sleeve. 'What have I done to him, oh my God, what *could* I have done to him!' Ricardo tried to calm her, but she paid no attention to him. 'He never stops needling me, ever, as if he had nothing else to do!'

I murmured a few consoling words and said that

Rafael often acted up, without meaning anything by it. . . .

'God knows why he's got it in for me. Why does he want to embitter my life? . . . Jesus, as if it were a crime to love your husband!'

We finally managed to get her in the car. During the drive she kept on crying, and Ricardo looked unhappy and stroked her hair. Loles and I didn't say a word. As they got out, Ana turned to Loles and heaved a sigh. 'Where do you want us to drop you off, child?'

'Oh, any place. Go on toward your house. That way I can stay a while longer with you both.'

'That's absurd,' Ana said. 'You won't find a taxi there.'

'I don't care. I'll walk back. I love walking at night.'

'Alvaro, tell her not to act like a child.'

'I want to enjoy being with you as long as possible. You're the most intelligent and marvellous people I've ever known. How can you expect me to feel sleepy after meeting you?'

Ana laughed, and Loles hugged her and said she'd never part with the earrings. The alcohol didn't dull my reflexes, and I was driving at more than fifty through the neighborhood streets. In front of our apartment house I braked suddenly.

'Good night,' I said to Loles.

Ana and she kissed again, and then Ana suddenly turned to me. 'Why don't you take Loles home?'

'I'd rather walk,' Loles protested.

'Don't be stupid. Alvaro will be happy to take you.'

'No, no,' she said. 'You can't imagine what this day means to me. I'm as awake as if I'd drunk a quart of coffee. . . . I need to be by myself.'

She got away from us at a run, and we went into the lobby without a word. As we were going up in the elevator, Ana pushed the stop button. 'Go on, what are you waiting for?' she said. 'There's still time.'

'Time for what?'

'Why did you refuse to take her home? Because of me?'

'If you think I've fallen in love with her, you're wrong,' I answered.

She looked for the key in her handbag and murmured, 'Are you sure?'

There was a vial of Alka-Seltzer on the night table, and she handed me a glass of water without a word. Bed was infinitely sweet after so many hours of tension and fatigue. Ana looked sad and distracted, and lay down at my side without looking at me.

'You feel better?'

'A little tired, that's all.'

'Sleep if you like, but just let me say one thing. . . . This is the last time I'm going out with you.'

'I don't understand.'

'You don't understand?' Ana sat up suddenly and looked at me angrily. 'Did you see yourself for a moment while we were eating?'

'Me? Why?'

'You can't have the least idea of how boring you get when you're with us. . . . It's unbearable, I swear, really unbearable. I'm horrified that people may think I'm living with a mute.'

'What do you want me to do? Tell jokes?'

'You know very well that's not what I meant. You don't care a bit for your friends, and you let them know it every moment you're with them. If you're bored with us, go your own way. But if you're not, try to make an effort. . . .'

'I've been making an effort for quite a while now, Ana.'

'I know that girls like Loles adore you as if you were the Holy Sacrament, but if you're going to live with me, I won't let you give in to your moods. You're not an old man yet, you know.'

Since I said nothing, she leaned towards me and caressed me tenderly. 'Forgive me for saying these things to you, darling. I'd rather you got mad at me than see you act like the village idiot. You used to be interested in other people. Now anything that isn't connected with your work bores you. Even when you're being charming and funny you seem to be doing it as an obligation. A moment later you're back in your shell and no one can get you out, not even by force.'

With my head on her breast, I answered that moral energy that remains unused turns into neurasthenia. The contrast between the subject and the painting, dreams and reality, is so dizzying that people like Rafael, Ricardo and me eventually doubt our own senses. I said we were slowly going crazy, and I didn't see how the process could be stopped. I said all this mechanically, as if someone else were talking. Ana looked at me with her beautiful dark eyes, and now and then nodded. 'Sleep, darling. We'll talk tomorrow.'

The next day the phone had been ringing for some time before Ana picked up the receiver. She answered in a sleepy voice and passed it to me with a sigh. 'It's Loles.'

My head throbbed with weariness, and I sat down on the side of the bed, my legs hanging over. 'What's the matter?' I said.

There was a long silence, and a childish voice murmured, 'Nothing.'

'You've woken us up. What do you want?'

'To listen to your voice.' Loles stopped again for a few

seconds. 'I haven't slept a wink all night. After I left you, I walked all the way to the port and spent the time counting the stars. . . .'

'What?'

'They're really pretty. I went down to the breakwater and argued with them. With the Big Bear and Arcturus and Cassiopeia and Vega de la Lira and Pegasus. . . .'

'Where are you calling from?'

'I've been at a darling bar for the last two hours. They've got thousands of barrels of wine and a showcase with trophies of the Pigeon Breeders' Federation of Spain. Don José Morenilla's dove Sultan won two silver cups and is the favorite for the next. . . .'

'Listen, what's the matter with you? Aren't you feeling well?'

'On the contrary, I feel better than ever. Everyone here adores me. A Basque pelota player . . .'

'What did you same the name of the bar is?'

'. . . has treated me to two cazallas and wants to take me to his apartment. The poor boy is out on the street now looking for a taxi to . . .'

'What street?'

'I'm happy, Alvaro, terribly happy. I've made friends with the stars and a pelota player. Do you know any pelota players? Mine is named Ricardo Segundo, like the king in Shakespeare. Isn't that wonderful?'

'Loles!'

'It's marvellous to hear your voice. All night I've been thinking about the fellow shackled to the window. . . . If we could be useful . . .'

'Tell me where you are.'

There was a few seconds' pause, then I heard Loles' high-pitched voice and a deeper one, a man's.

'What's happening?'

'There's someone here who wants to talk to you. A veteran of . . .'

'Hello?'

'Who's on the phone?' the man asked.

'To whom am I speaking?' I asked.

'Are you this girl's father?'

'No.'

'Well, do you know her?'

'Yes.'

'You'd better come and get her right away. She's a bit tipsy, and I can't keep her here in the bar much longer. The police, you understand?'

'Absolutely. What's your address?'

The owner of the bar gave it to me, and Loles got on the phone again.

'I want to buy a dove, Alvaro. A champion dove like Don José's. . . .'

'Listen to me carefully. I'm coming right now to pick you up. Try not to drink any more, and above all don't leave there.'

'And the pelota player? What do I do with the pelota player?'

'Tell him you've phoned your father and to go to hell. I'll be with you in fifteen minutes.'

'You're an angel, Alvaro. Your wife and you are . . .'

'Tell the owner I want to talk to him.'

'The veteran?'

'Yes.'

Loles murmured something, and the man got on the phone again.

'Listen to me,' I said. 'I'm a lawyer and I warn you that if the situation gets more complicated, you can get into lots of trouble. Don't let her leave the bar for any reason, understand?'

'Yes, sir.'

'I'm getting my car right now. If something happens before I get there, I'll hold you responsible.'

I finally hung up, and for a few seconds I looked at Ana's tense, tired face.

'What's happened to her?'

'Nothing. She's had too much to drink and is talking nonsense.'

'What do you intend to do?'

'For the moment, just get her out in the fresh air. As soon as she's better, I'll take her home.' I started to get dressed and then added, 'Lucky she thought of phoning. In the state she's in she'd do anything.'

Ana said nothing. In the bathroom, I wet my head under the faucet and combed my hair quickly. While I was putting on a tie, she got up suddenly and gave me a rancorous look.

'Why didn't you drive her home as I told you to? Did you want to make her suffer?'

'Don't talk nonsense, Ana.'

'It's not nonsense. You wanted to make her fall in love with you and you've succeeded. . . . Are you happy now?'

'I don't have time to talk now. What you're imagining or assuming isn't true. We'll talk when I get back.'

'All right, all right,' said Ana. 'Whatever you say.'

I ran down the stairs, got to the car, and then realized I'd forgotten the car key and went back to get it. Ana had shut herself up in the bathroom. I was about to call her and cover up my forgetfulness with some tender gesture, but at the last moment I didn't do it.

I drove down Urgel, and at the Ronda de San Pablo I continued via Paralelo and Paseo Colón. Despite the early hour, the trolleys were already jammed with people going swimming at San Sebastian. It was Sunday, and the stores and factories were closed. I parked the car at a corner of Almirante Cervera and immediately found the bar.

Loles was sitting in the back room with two strangers. Her charming, young-boy's profile contrasted with the hard, weather-beaten faces of the men. When I entered, she was staring up at the trophies in the showcase, looking sad and crestfallen. When she saw me, she perked up.

'At last,' she said. 'I was telling these two guys that you're the most seductive person I've ever met. My friend Alvaro . . . I want to introduce the champion. . . .'

'Ricardo Segundo, at your service.'

The pelota player put out his hand, but I acted as if I didn't see it and turned to the other man.

'Are you the owner?'

'Yes, sir.'

'Come with me a moment. I want a word with you.'

Loles looked at me with misty eyes and made a childish face.

'Kiss me Alvaro. Kiss me in front of them so that . . .'

'Wait a moment.'

'No, now. Ricardo Segundo has invited us to his place. He has a prize dove, too. It's a male. A female gets a teeny wire with a feather twisted around one leg and when they let her go, the males . . .'

'How much do I owe you?' I said to the owner as we walked toward the bar.

'Thirty pesetas fifty and whatever else you'd care to give.'

I gave him a bill for twenty *duros*, and without waiting for change I went back and took Loles by the hand.

'Look at the trophies. The ones on the top shelf belong to Don José Morenilla . . .'

'Don't forget your purse.'

'Are we leaving already?' she said. She looked pain-
fully surprised, and she pointed to the pelota player with
one finger. 'Ricardo Segundo wants to show us his
pigeons. He's a charter member of the Pigeon Breeders'
Federation of Spain and says that . . .'

'Come on, don't dawdle.'

I managed to get her outside, and in the street she
threw her arms around my neck and tried to kiss me.

'I'm happy, Alvaro. . . . I've never loved anyone this
way. I was telling the stars, if Alvaro gets them to free
the man at the window . . .'

'Keep walking. We're almost there.'

'I've been drinking to lose my shyness, understand?
Ricardo Segundo wanted to kiss me on the mouth, and I
kept thinking: this is the character in Shakespeare.'

Passers-by stopped to look at us, and as I manoeuvred
her into the car they formed a ring around us.

'Why are they looking at me?' Loles said. 'Do they
know it's the happiest day of my life?'

'Yes,' I said. 'That must be why they're looking.'

As I drove off I looked at myself in the mirror and
noticed beads of sweat on my forehead. Loles had leaned
her head on my shoulder in a gesture of abandon. Her
lips instinctively searched for mine. I thought of the
cheap passes the man in the bar must have made, and my
heart started to pound.

At the end of the Paseo Nacional, I went on toward the
tower and up to the highway along the breakwater. Near
the lighthouse there was parking space. The waves were
beating against the cement wall, and down on the rocks
many fishermen were patiently awaiting a bite, fishing
pole in hand.

I went to get some coffee at the restaurant and made
her drink it after having dissolved two aspirins in it.

Loles leaned her elbows on the parapet. The wind tossed her hair, and she looked out at the sea without daring to raise her eyes.

'Are you angry?' she asked.

'You've given Ana and me a terrible fright. What made you do it?'

'Tell me you're not furious with me.'

'I'm not furious with you, Loles, but don't do this again. . . . What kind of a face am I going to put on for your parents?'

'I felt so lucky. I would have slept with anyone just to be able to talk about you.'

'Promise me you'll be more reasonable from now on. . . . Ana must be terribly upset.'

'I know I shouldn't say certain things. If I hadn't been drinking, I wouldn't talk to you this way. Alvaro . . .'

'Yes.'

'Tell me you love me a little. Even if it's a lie. Tell me.'

'Ana and I love you very much.'

'No, speak for yourself.'

'I love you, Loles.' My temples were throbbing again, and I lit a cigarette to avoid the temptation of her lips. 'Let's go now. Your parents may wake up any moment now. Don't make them suffer needlessly.'

Loles didn't move. Just half a mile from the coast there was an aircraft carrier of the American Sixth Fleet, and she was staring at its gray silhouette that looked like a menacing, metallic grasshopper.

'Last year, on my mother's saint's day, I met a Danish couple in the Plaza Real and I brought them home for dinner. Papa couldn't stop saying, "They're the ugliest couple I've ever seen"; he said it in Catalan so they wouldn't understand. And when they left, he said:

"Well, let's see if you'll bring some Tibetans home next time." Since that day they're not surprised at anything. If you like, I can phone them and . . .'

'Listen carefully,' I interrupted. 'I'm a respectful and respectable man, and I don't want it said that I've taken to ravishing little girls. You're getting in the car right now and we're going straight to your house.'

Loles obeyed. Her eyes obstinately looked at some fixed point ahead of her, and as we drove back along the breakwater she began to sob.

'Then it was a lie?'

'What's the matter? Can you tell me why you're crying?'

'I thought you were being serious. . . .'

'Serious about what?'

'When you said you loved me. Oh, why did you fool me?'

'I've told you the simple truth, Loles. Don't force me to say it again.'

She faced me with a radiant expression. Her tears disappeared instantly.

'It's been a really marvellous night. We shouldn't go to sleep ever, Alvaro. My conscience always bothers me when I go to bed. If we could only live a thousand years. . . . But our time's so fleeting. . . .'

'Fleeting is the right word. For once you're saying something sensible.' The image of the pelota player tormented me, and the discovery that I was jealous was the final bitterness. 'I'm barely thirty, and I feel at the end of my rope. Just the opposite of what's happening to you has been happening to me these last two years. I should spend all my time sleeping. It would be time gained.'

'Gained? What for?'

'I don't know, Loles. Time wears us out little by little. ... I'd like to be twenty and have your capacity for enthusiasm. That's why you attract me: because you're still intact, and when I'm with you things seem new.'

'Only because of that?'

'Yes, only because of that. Because it's convenient.'

Loles wasn't listening to me, so I stopped my lecture. We were driving up Layetana, and as soon as we passed the main police headquarters, I turned toward Urquinaona and Paseo San Juan.

'How are you feeling now?' I asked when we arrived.

'Perfect.' She twisted the rear-view mirror to look at herself and made a childish pout. 'Do you think they'll guess we're in love?'

'Stop talking nonsense.' I had parked at the curb and taken out the ignition key. 'Come on, I'll go with you.'

'Wouldn't it be better if I went up alone?'

'Don't be a child,' I answered. 'I want to go with you.'

She finished combing her hair in the mirror, and we kissed quickly. In the elevator, we thought up a plausible excuse: Loles had lost her keys, and in order not to wake them up in the middle of the night, she had decided to stay at our house. Her mother opened the door just as usual.

'Hello,' she said. 'Have you had a good time?'

Neither of us said a word, surprised, and while she preceded us down a narrow hall, she explained that Ana had phoned an hour earlier to reassure them and had said that she had forced Loles to stay with her.

'My daughter can't stop talking about you two. She's in love with you and your wife. It's all she talks about.'

'We love her very much, too,' I said.

She insisted on giving me a cup of coffee, and for some ten minutes I had to listen to a lecture on the dangers of

modernism and the need for moral rearmament. Finally,
I managed to get away, and Loles escorted me to the door
and took advantage of the dark foyer to kiss me. Out on
the street, I felt full of nervous energy. All the people
dressed in their Sunday best and busily coming and going
made me feel vaguely that it was all unreal. It was beginning to get hot, and I sought out the shade of a bar and
drank a second cup of coffee.

It was only five past ten, and after having gone
through so much that morning, the prospect of a day
hardly yet begun depressed me. My earlier excitement
had disappeared and been replaced by a vague anxiety, a
nostalgia for some unrealizable dream. Behind the bar
there was a mirror with an advertisement for Cinzano
and an announcement of the final eliminations for the
Generalissimo Cup. For a long time I spied on myself in
the mirror, as if I were some stranger. I looked pale, I
had circles under my eyes, and a twenty-four-hour beard
made me look older. While I was waiting for change, I
decided to go into a barbershop.

There was one open a few steps away, and I sat down
with the other customers and watched the bright sunlight
and the activity on the street. When my turn came, I felt
terribly tired. The barber began to soap my face, and I
abandoned myself with pleasure to the soapy brush and
the light touch of the blade. It was wonderful to close my
eyes, smell the aroma of stinging lotion, feel his gentle
fingers and the air's fresh caress. The pleasure lasted so
short a time that it made me feel sad. As I paid, I looked
with envy at the line of those who had come after I had.
If it had been possible, I would have sat down and waited
my turn again.

I meant to call Ana immediately, but when I got to
the car I changed my mind and dropped in on the

reporter for *El Caso*. He opened the door himself; he was still in a robe and slippers, and he led me to a small room full of books and files.

'Did you find out anything?' I asked.

He fumbled in his wallet and took out a piece of paper with some typing on it. 'José Contreras Fernández,' he read. 'Born in Caravaca, province of Murcia, 16 February, 1928. ... Son of Francisco Contreras López and María Fernández Castro. Profession, day laborer. Married 11 June ...'

'May I see?' He handed me the paper, and I read it quickly. 'Confirmed petty thief. Sought 7–11–1957 by the Provincial Court of Murcia for stealing cattle belonging to Don ... Sought by the Provincial Court of Alicante for ...'

'Good, good, that's all I wanted to know.'

'I talked to him for a while, while he was being photographed. He's a poor devil, can't read or write.'

'Do you think I can do something?'

'That's for you to decide. Look at the record. . . . In my opinion, he'll get five years, with or without a lawyer.'

I passed him my pack of Pall Malls, and when he had given me a light he talked about our college days. 'I immediately went in for journalism. A law career has greater potential, but there're damn few openings. Unless, of course, you're talented and have a rich family like you.'

'It's all a matter of luck,' I answered.

'Don't be modest, you can't convince me that way. I know only too well the reputation you've got as a terror in court. You're a hard man, and you can't be bought.'

He walked me to the stairs, taking my arm familiafly. When I reached the street, the sun's glare dazzled me.

Cars sped by. I decided not to go home yet and sat on the terrace of a café. It seemed to me that people were walking by unnecessarily fast. The waiter brought me a cuba libre with gin, and I felt better after I had drunk it. I drove up Balmes slowly until I got to Diagonal.

Ana had gone out. The room had been tidied, and I lay down on the bed and waited. A radio somewhere was broadcasting high mass from the cathedral. Sleep enveloped me like vertigo, and I closed my eyes.

The phone's ringing woke me, and I instinctively looked at the clock. It was ten past three.

'Alvaro?' Her voice seemed far away, mixed up with indistinct noises.

'Where are you?'

'I'm with Paco Iruña, outside Barcelona. We've stopped to eat at a stand. Have you been back long?'

'Yes. . . . I'd fallen asleep.'

'I've left you a chicken wing and some fried potatoes in the refrigerator. If you want anything more, look in the cupboard. . . .'

'I'm not hungry.'

'Are you in a bad mood?'

'Me? Why do you say that?'

'I don't know, your voice sounds strange.'

'I'm half asleep.'

'Well, rest then. . . . It's a gorgeous day; we'll probably be back late. Are you thinking of going out?'

'Perhaps.'

'If you go out, let me know. Did everything work out all right about Loles?'

'Very well, thanks.'

'You can tell me all about it tonight.'

'All right.'

' 'Bye, Alvaro.'

'Have a good time.'

After I had hung up, I opened the window wide and listened to the confused noise of conversations and radio programs that came up from the patio. My body ached, and I took a cold shower. I found the chicken and the potatoes in the refrigerator. There was also half a bottle of Monopol, and I drank it all without realizing it. It was the first time I had eaten alone in many years. The noise of the refrigerator buzzed in my ears, and I drew the blind to keep out the glare of the noon.

When I had finished, I called Rafael's house. The maid answered and said they both had gone out with the boy and wouldn't return until after supper.

'Don't you know where they've gone?'

'No, sir.'

For a moment I thought of phoning Ricardo, but the thought of seeing Tere depressed me. I put the receiver back on the hook before I finished dialing and straightened up my desk. When I finished that I was panting with fatigue. I was afraid Loles would appear any moment, and I decided to take a ride in the car.

It was a real summer day, and you literally could breathe the atmosphere of excitement that precedes the holiday season. I drove along Infanta Carlota as far as the Plaza de España, and then continued toward Paralelo and the pier at San Beltrán. People returning from the beach pressed against each other on the trolley platforms. On the highway to the free port there were innumerable bicycles. When I got to the spot where the man had been handcuffed, I stopped and looked at the bars on the window. Bathers were walking about in noisy groups, and the radio at the eating stand nearby was broadcasting the semi-finals. The customers listened without interrupting their card games. In the patio there was a shallow boat, and the owner was explaining to a boy the right way to catch eels. 'When the season begins, I'll take you with me some night,' he promised.

I drank a cuba libre with gin and headed toward the cemetery. The bar at the trolley stop was jammed and the Andalusians were also playing cards and listening to the radio.

'Two to zero in favor of Madrid.'

I leaned on one end of the bar. The girl came and went, working hard, but she smiled flirtatiously when she saw me.

'The usual?'

'That's right.'

She mixed the cuba libre and, after serving it, stood in front of me smoothing her hair.

'You've come alone?'

'That's right.'

'And the young lady?'

'She had a date,' I said.

'That man who wanted to talk to you was around this morning. . . .'

'What man?'

'The big one with the scar.'

'Zurguena?'

'Yes, sir.'

'Do you know what he wanted?'

'To bother you, I suppose. He's always in trouble.'

'Did he leave any message?'

'No. He asked me if I knew your address. When I told him you were here yesterday, it made him mad.'

I drank half the glass in one gulp. The girl remained in front of me, her arms akimbo.

'What's his address?' I said.

'Whose?'

'That fellow's.'

'Are you going to see him?'

'I might as well stretch my legs. Is it far from here?'

'I'm not sure. Ask at those huts. They'll tell you.'

She turned her back on me with obvious disapproval, and when I had finished the cuba libre I left three *duros* on the bar and crossed the esplanade of the cemetery.

In summer the people of the neighborhood practically lived out on the streets. The kids were running around barefoot. I stopped at a group of women. 'Do you know a man called Zurguena?'

'Go straight ahead and turn at the second road to the right. You'll find him right away.'

The radio was still broadcasting the soccer match. From their seats along the walk, the radio listeners watched me out of the corner of their eyes. On a second path I ran into a seller of ices. The children thronged around his cart and sucked ices avidly.

'Does someone called Zurguena live around here?'

The boy I asked pointed to a closed hut. 'It's over there,' he said, and added, 'He's gone.'

'Do you know where?'

'No, sir.'

I knocked on the door but there was no answer. Some neighbors came over and questioned the boy. 'He may be at Casa Valero,' said one. 'On Sunday he usually goes to his brother-in-law's.'

'Where did you say?'

'I don't remember the number of the house, but you can't miss it. Do you know the dance hall?'

'Yes.'

'Well, it's just behind it. If you walk through the cemetery ...'

'I've brought a car.'

'In that case I'll accompany you, and you won't get lost.'

'Don't bother, thanks. I'll manage by myself.'

'It's no bother. Actually, I was thinking of going by there. . . . If you'll wait a minute, I'll get my jacket.'

The man disappeared inside a hut and came back with a jacket thrown over his shoulders. On the lapel there was a black ribbon.

'Whenever you say.'

His neighbors' glances followed us, and some winked at him and asked if he was going to the Ritz.

'Are you a friend of Zurguena's?' he asked.

'I met him a couple of months ago. He used to come to the bar often. The one at the stop, you know.'

'He's a good guy. Everyone in the neighborhood liked him.'

While we drove up Montjuich, he explained that Zurguena was a good friend to all and shared his bread with others. 'A little crazy, that's true, but he'd never harm a fly.'

Past the stadium, I took the avenue on the left and parked behind the taxi stop. The loudspeakers of the eating stand were playing a slow number. The couples on the dance floor held each other tight and those standing under the enormous vines that covered the summer terrace looked enviously at the dancers. A guard at the door kept the children out. My companion pushed his way through and asked various persons for Zurguena. Soldiers, waitresses, Andalusians with thin mustaches and nylon shirts sweated, turned, pressed, and jostled each other to the beat of a soggy, hermaphroditic voice, while family groups drank jugs of wine mixed with soda water and unpacked enormous sandwiches of roasted sausages and pieces of bread soaked in tomato sauce.

After making a tour of the dance floor, we tried the bar. Zurguena wasn't there either, and my companion talked to the owner a bit. When we left, he said that according to the owner he'd been by in the morning with some other man and asked for a loan. 'Let's go to the brother-in-law's place. Maybe he's there.'

I followed him along a muddy lane toward the ravine. This search for Zurguena had somehow become something vital for me. It seemed to me that if I found him, my anxiety would disappear at once. Some huts in that section had tiny gardens, and we stopped before one decorated with morning-glories in hanging flower-pots. A man was resting in the shade of a fig tree. My companion greeted him with a wave of his hand.

'What brings you here, José?' said the man.

'Let me tell you.' José had a burnt-out cigarette in one corner of his mouth, and he lit it with his lighter. 'This gentleman is looking for your brother-in-law, and I thought perhaps you could tell him where he is.'

'I don't know where he is,' answered the man. His crafty little eyes looked me up and down. 'Do you want something from him?'

I told him about my conversation with the girl at the bar, and his eyes softened a bit. 'Is your name Alvaro by any chance?'

'Yes.'

'My God! I can't tell you how many times he's mentioned your name to me, and your friends' names too. This very morning before he left . . .' The man abruptly lowered his voice. 'I'm going to tell you something in confidence that's just between us, understand?' José agreed with a nod. 'My brother-in-law has taken off for France to look for work, without a passport or any papers. . . .'

'When?'

'Just a few hours ago. He bought a ticket to Figueras and from there he plans to walk cross-country.'

'It's absurd. If he had told me in time I could have fixed it legally. I have friends here and in Paris who . . .'

'My brother-in-law had been looking for you for weeks. He even went to the Palace of Justice to ask for you there. Since he didn't have your address . . .'

'Isn't there any way of catching up with him?'

'Forget it! God knows where he is by this time.'

'Didn't he leave you an address?'

'None, no, sir. He went with a man who's got a contact, a guide who's already slipped someone from our town into France. He promised to send word if everything went well.'

The man stopped talking, and the sick feeling I'd been experiencing for the last few months turned into an acute, painful pang of impotence. After we discussed Zurguena's reasons for leaving illegally, the conversation began to falter, and I invited them to have a drink with me at Casa Valero. Finally, I got them to walk with me to the car and we said good-bye.

'I'll come back one of these days,' I promised. They waved good-bye, and I stepped on the accelerator.

When I got home, it was past eight. Ana had just fin-ished showering and came into the room wrapped in a beach robe. Her beautiful features were veiled by a shadow of sadness.

'Loles called you. She wants you to phone her.'

She touched my cheek with her lips and began comb-ing her hair at the dressing table. Her back was to me but I could feel her looking at me in the mirror.

'Alvaro,' she said, after a moment's silence.

'Yes.'

She went on combing her hair calmly, and her voice

sounded profoundly sad. 'Paco has fallen in love with me.'

The sweet, macabre music of impotence cradled me again and became one with me. 'How about you? Do you love him?'

Our glances met for an instant. Ana moved her lips and made a helpless gesture. 'I don't know, Alvaro,' she said. 'I don't know.'

From the bed, I could see the desk, the Isabelline chest of drawers, the screen made out of *New Yorker* covers. Ana's hand mechanically smoothed her hair and suddenly she pulled one out and examined it in amazement.

'A gray hair.'

She came over to show it to me and brought her mouth close to mine.

'You're right, Alvaro,' she said. 'We're getting old.'

Third

IT ALL STARTED because of the letters. Before we went to bed Juan said, 'Are you leaving them with me?'

'If you like,' I answered.

He put them away in his desk, and we didn't discuss the subject again. From that time on he couldn't sleep, and he had no appetite. His life continued the same on the surface, but the way he looked was a bad sign. He hardly talked, and kept looking at me in a funny way. Finally, I asked him what was wrong with him.

'With me?' His surprise seemed genuine.

'Yes, you. For some time now I've noticed a change in you. You look as if you were mulling something over and didn't want to tell me about it.'

'No, nothing like that,' he said. 'I've worked hard this winter. It must be fatigue.'

That same day we decided on a change of scenery. Juan had turned in his final urbanization plans to the construction company, and he was free until the fall. The heat in Barcelona was killing. Most of our friends were vacationing on the Costa Brava or at Sitges. Jaime and his wife were still in Tossa, and we packed our bags without saying good-bye to anyone.

Juan brought along a briefcase filled with projects. I remember that near Peñíscola he parked the Seat on the shoulder of the road. A group of workers was digging a ditch among the pines. With an ironic gesture he pointed out the company's new chalets to me.

'All those messes are my creations. Then the Valencians come along and paint them in loud colors. Ah, and I'd forgotten something – all the furniture is cherry wood, and in every dining room there's a plaster cast of The Last Supper.'

'It's not your fault that people are stupid and demand those things,' I said.

'You're wrong,' he answered. 'I'm the only stupid one.'

The conversation ended there. Later, during the weeks that followed, I told myself I should have said more, but it was already too late. Juan had become withdrawn and refused to talk about his job. For a month and a half we covered the beaches of Alicante one by one. We sunbathed from sunup to sundown and amused ourselves comparing our tans. He liked the sea air. We ate sardines and baked pimentos at eating stands on the shore and washed them down with claret of the region. Juan seemed self-absorbed and only talked with ease about wine and politics. Some nights, he would suddenly go off and leave me in the company of some stranger. When he returned, he'd always ask if I had enjoyed myself. He did this to prove to himself that he was free, and I couldn't think of anything that would cure him. The briefcase was left forgotten in the car, and we both pretended that it didn't exist.

At the end of six weeks, I began to miss our life in Barcelona and made a mental list of good reasons for returning. Juan's healthy look was deceiving, and I was afraid of this prolonged, lazy holiday and his constant use of sleeping pills. The vacation had solved nothing; only work would help him regain his balance. When I said as much, he agreed with me.

'But it's too soon to go back home yet,' he added. 'How about going a little farther?'

'Farther? Where?'

'I don't know,' he murmured. 'Some place where there're no Germans. Just for a couple of weeks more. . . .'

It was September, and the season was ending. On the road, caravans of foreign cars were heading north. In Guardamar, vacationers danced on an improvised dance floor under the shade of eucalyptuses. A haze slowly crept over the sky, and as we crossed the marshes I saw clouds gathering and threatening to blot out the sky. Salt gathered in blinding white piles on the drying floors and shone as if with an incandescent light. Juan drove fast and didn't stop until Mar Menor.

When we arrived there, the town looked abandoned. The streets were empty, and the car raised a cloud of dust behind us. Juan parked by the church, and we got out to look at the sea. The place lacked a proper beach, and the cabañas jutted out into the water on rickety wooden pontoons. Little waves died out slowly at the edge of the pier. Fishing smacks anchored at buoys rocked lazily. The horizon cut the sand bar, and the sea stretched out, dirty and foggy, as far as you could see.

'A good place,' said Juan. 'You can work here in peace.'

The scene evoked a faded chromo of a vacation scene, and I watched the monotonous, languid flight of the seagulls with apprehension. There was absolutely no one on the pier. The backless mosaic benches, the doors and windows boarded up to protect them from the wind helped create a nineteenth-century atmosphere. We drove through the dusty streets until we found the hotel.

It was a deserted building, gray like its neighbors, with a row of balconies that overlooked the sea. The owner met us with an apron tied round his waist, and went to take a look at his register before giving us a room.

'Will you be staying long?'

'We don't know,' said Juan. 'It depends on the weather.'

'September is magnificent here. Much better than August; there's less noise. In the summer you can't walk a step, so many people come down from Madrid and other cities. Just imagine on the Virgin's day we had to have two orchestras.'

'Do foreigners come?'

'Foreigners and people from all over Spain. But the greatest number come from Murcia.' He corrected himself. 'From Murcia and the countryside around it.'

The furniture in our room amounted to two beds, a chest, a table, and chairs. The owner helped us carry our bags upstairs, and then we went out to take a walk around the town.

As it got darker, the sea seemed to thicken. From the dock of the hotel we could make out the keys half hidden by the mist. A fishing boat headed into the wind and crossed close to the bow of a tiny rowboat. The fishing boat was heading for San Javier, hugging the coast, and after it passed I turned to watch the rowboat. A man was rowing against the current, fighting the choppy water. As he turned to windward, I saw a woman's silhouette against the stern: a tanned girl, dressed in a dark jersey and toreador pants. When they moored at the dock, the man put away the oars and helped her get off.

At supper we saw her again in the dining room. She was the only other guest at the hotel, and when she sat down at the next table, she said good evening. The owner brought her a bottle of wine already opened. She said she wasn't hungry and complained of the strong wind from the sea.

'I almost got seasick this afternoon. Lucky I hadn't had anything to drink.'

'You'll see how sunny it'll be tomorrow. The wind will change at dawn and drive the clouds away.'

'I hope so.'

'Of course, my girl, of course. The southeaster never lasts long here. Tomorrow you'll be able to go out to the sandbar.'

The owner returned to his place behind the bar and watched us, his elbows on the little door of the counter. When she had finished the bottle, the girl asked for another; but she left immediately without tasting it and said she was going to play dominoes in town. The owner's eyes followed her. While he took away the dishes, he explained to us that she was Portuguese.

'Her father is an admiral in the Navy and has travelled all over the world. Still, when he stops here he always says, "The best beaches I know are Miami and this one." The girl has been spending her summers with us since she was ten.'

'Did she come alone?'

'Yes, alone. The air here is very good for the health. You'll see children arrive here skinny, wasting away, and in a few days you wouldn't recognize them – they've grown so and put on so much weight. It's not that I want to make claims or publicity for the hotel, no sir, but it *is* a magnificent place.'

That night we both slept like logs. When I opened the window of our room, it was after ten. The horizon was as foggy as the evening before, and I looked at the deserted piers and the dead, flat sea for a long while. Some women were chatting below, sitting in the sand at the foot of the pier. The water scarcely reached their waists, and they rocked back and forth at the mercy of the waves.

Juan was still groggy from his sleeping pills, and I

went down to the dining room. The owner was grinding coffee behind the bar. He smiled when he saw me.

'Did you rest well?'

'Very well.'

'The weather isn't good yet,' he said. 'The wind has settled in and the boats haven't been able to take off to fish.'

'It's all the same to me,' I answered. 'We'll swim at another beach somewhere.'

'If you're not going too far, you can rent a boat.'

The Portuguese girl had already had breakfast. On her table there was an empty cup and a plate with crullers. Juan didn't show up until a half hour later.

'Where are we going?' he asked.

'To some beach or other. I'd like to lie on the sand and read.'

We went out to the pier. Some kids were running along the boardwalk. The bathers were paddling on the pontoons, and two old men were stretching out a line of nets in front of the fish-shop. Juan looked around eagerly and assured me that he'd never felt better in his life.

'I feel like leaving those bastards in the lurch and settling here to live,' he said.

The fishermen sat around waiting on the stone benches next to the shed. A boy sat on the ground straightening the rushes at the neck of the fisherman's trap. Juan went over to watch, and a young-looking man came over to meet us. I recognized him because of his beret; he was the man who'd been rowing the boat.

'It's used for catching eels,' he said. 'They enter through the opening and then can't get out.'

Juan passed him his pack of Chesterfields. The man gave him a light, shielding it with his hands.

'Do you want to go out ?'

'We'd like to go out to the sandbar.'

'You can't today. When the wind blows from inland, there're too many swells. You can't tell from here. But you'd notice it all right if we went out.'

'Where can we go ?'

'Toward Los Urrutias. If we go out away from the coast, the sea gets nasty immediately.'

We accompanied him to the dock, and the man took the oars aboard and held me as I jumped onto the seat. Juan and I sat in front of him. We were in the lee of the wind, and the boat hardly moved. The man put in the oars, carefully fitting them in the oarlocks, and we rowed out.

The town slept a gray, dead sleep. A governess in a headdress and a white apron waved good-bye to us from one of the docks. The bathers were still paddling next to the pier, and the man explained that they spent the summer like that and could never make up their minds to get on a boat.

'Why ?' I asked.

'People from inland are scared of the water.' He shrugged his shoulders. 'Out on the sandbar there are some very nice beaches, and they don't even come to see them, if only out of curiosity. People from Madrid are different. They enjoy the sea.'

He asked if we were staying at the hotel, and I said yes.

'Señor Joaquín, the owner, is a friend of mine. Before he lost his wife he often used to go fishing.'

'How is his business ?'

'During the season he gets by. The hotel fills up in August. Then he closes it in October and doesn't open it again until summer.'

We hugged the coast, and he pointed with his arm at the installations at the seaplane base. 'They've practically abandoned it. Now most of the personnel is in San Javier.'

During the war, however, several dozen seaplanes were stationed there, and the technicians built an airfield. 'They call it the Russian's Camp,' he added.

We were going upwind, and the boat pitched. Between the seaplane base and Los Urrutias there stretched an ocher valley dotted with palm trees and windmills. Every once in a while the wind would raise a cloud of orange dust.

'If you like fishing, I'll take you out in my motorboat. Last week we put it in dry-dock to get the bottom scraped, but it'll be ready tomorrow and we can let the nets down.'

'How do you fish?' said Juan. 'With a gang line?'

'No, around here we usually go for giltheads or mullets. With gill nets or *pasantanas*.'

The breeze stiffened, and waves dashed against the keel and splashed us. The man laughed and said we should move to the seat at the bow. In sight of Los Urrutias we came alongside another boat. The rower – an old fisherman – steered with an oar from the stern and greeted our friend in a hoarse voice.

'Who is he?' Juan asked.

Without missing a stroke, the man explained that he was the father of the boy who had been weaving the fish traps in the fish-shop. 'In town they call him Morillo. We've all got nicknames here.'

'And you? What do they call you?'

'They call me Isabelo,' he said with a smile.

As we approached the beach the wind died down. The waves broke, low and flat, and let you look through to the pebbles on the bottom. Then, as the wind fell, the waves disappeared completely, and you couldn't see a ripple on the surface of the water.

The boat plowed, almost touching bottom with its keel, and Isabelo stopped rowing, took out one of the oars, and started slowly to land the boat, using the oar like a pole. When the boat hit bottom, he secured a hemp rope to a belaying pin and threw out the anchor.

I took off my pants and blouse, and Isabelo helped me climb down from the boat. The water hardly reached my thighs. Juan had also undressed and suggested that we go to town to drink beer.

'No thanks,' said the man. 'I'll wait for you here.'

'Do you know a bar?'

'On the highway there's one, but you should dress to go there. Otherwise the Civil Guard will fine you.'

Isabelo handed us our shirts and sat down on top of the hatch with his legs hanging over. Juan made him take a pack of Chesterfields. The shore of the beach was covered with dry seaweed, and it gave as I walked. The sun's glare hurt my eyes.

In Los Urrutias there wasn't a soul – as if its inhabitants had moved out after the last storm. The doors and windows of the houses were boarded up. The only notes of color were the street lamps and some palm trees here and there, withered and yellow.

'Do you think we'll find some place open?' I said.

Juan seemed happy in the midst of that desolation. His vitality was always revived by poverty, and his eyes shone as they had on the afternoon he took me to Montjuich and got drunk with the men in some dive. His childhood had been that of a rich boy, all of whose tastes and whims were satisfied, and he was a stranger to sleepless nights and queues and scrambling for a crust of bread. I had known all that during the war years and the hard times that followed, and the mere recollection horrified me.

'Let's try,' he said.

I followed him through an alley to the first entrance hall we saw open. Inside, a little boy was plaiting hemp rope, and when we asked him the way, he got up and guided us to the highway. Near the corner there was a factory building with an advertisement for Pepsi Cola in the form of a bottle top.

'It's there,' he said, but he added, 'It's closed.'

'Isn't there any other?'

'No.'

We returned to the beach. Isabelo was smoking, looking out to the horizon, and we lay down on the dry seaweed along the shore. The old man's boat had disappeared from sight. The islands off Mar Menor emerged hazily through a thick mist, and for a few minutes I kept my eyes closed, thinking of Barcelona and our friends.

When I opened them, Juan was still stretched out at my side, and he turned his eyes away toward the sea.

'What are you doing?' I asked.

'Nothing,' he murmured. 'I was looking at you.'

He got up suddenly and added, 'Shall we go in?'

I dived into the water after him, and when we got to the boat we dressed, and Isabelo hoisted anchor. Again he manoeuvred with the oar to keep the boat's keel from scratching bottom, and when he could no longer touch bottom he fitted the oar in the oarlock and began to row slowly.

We skirted the coast, the wind at our stern and whitecaps on the water. Isabelo rowed contentedly. The boat seemed to glide over the water with each stroke. I asked him if he was married and he said yes.

'My wife has given me two kids, one boy, one girl.'

'Is she from this town?'

'Yes, ma'am. We all are in my family.'

He told us that he had never been out of the country except when he had served in the Navy.

While Señor Joaquín set our places at dinner, he told us that Isabelo had had a very hard time when his father died, but that for some time now things had been going better for him.

'His wife is very hard-working. He also works his brother-in-law's boat and now they go halves.'

'We're going out fishing with him tomorrow,' said Juan.

The Portuguese girl was eating at the next table, and she smiled at us. She was thin, with a pleasant face, and a hint of down above her lips. Señor Joaquín didn't take his eyes off her, and when we went up for our siesta, Juan said she had a lot of sex appeal.

'Why don't you run after her?' I told him.

'Wait,' he answered. 'Everything in due time.'

He threw himself on the bed, turning his back to me, and I closed the shutters. Then I lay down too. Flies buzzed about the room, and the heat was unbearable. The springs of Juan's mattress faithfully announced his every move. After a few minutes, I heard him call my name softly, but I didn't answer and pretended to be asleep.

At six we went out for a walk. The sky was still leaden, and out toward the sandbar thick clouds blocked the horizon and stretched out toward the islands like a trail of smoke. The pier and the docks were deserted. The waves kept the tied-up boats bobbing, and we stopped in front of the fish-shop to watch the sea.

'It's a very lively place,' I said.

Juan didn't answer, and I took his arm and leaned my head on his shoulder.

'Pay no attention to me, dear. I'm only talking for the sake of talking. It's all the same to me whether I'm here or some other place. What's important is for you to feel well and enjoy working.'

The Portuguese girl came along the street with some town boys. She was wearing tight jeans and a low-cut blouse, and she greeted us as she went by. Juan looked after her as she walked away.

'I may not look it, but I'm very jealous,' I said. 'If you show an interest in other women I get furious.'

'What do you want me to do? Not look at them?'

'No, dear, I didn't say that. Actually, I'm delighted. ... I only wanted to explain that we women like to call a spade a spade. If we're jealous, we confess it shamelessly. But no one ever knows what you men are thinking. If you talked a little more, I'm sure we'd get to understand each other.'

Juan made a vague grimace, and we returned to the hotel without saying a word, holding each other affectionately around the waist. The owner sat waiting for us in a wicker armchair next to the door.

'Ah! out for a walk?' Without waiting for an answer, he pointed to the sea and started to get up. 'See that clearing?'

'Yes?'

'That shows the wind is changing direction. The clouds will be gone by tomorrow.'

On top of the bar counter there was a sailor's cap from the crew of the *Lepanto*. Guessing that we would be curious, Señor Joaquín informed us that his son had arrived from Cartagena to spend the weekend.

'He was off duty and took this opportunity to get

away for a few hours. The minute he arrived he went out for a walk with María. . . . He works very fast, that boy.'

'María ?'

'The Portuguese girl. They've known each other since they were children.'

Later – since we made no comment – he said that his son had a very happy nature and was welcomed everywhere. In Cartagena he had made friends with important people, he said, and seldom set foot in the village now. He had bought himself two custom-made suits with his savings, a gold Duward watch, and a commando jacket. When he finished his tour of duty, he planned to get a job in some ministry in the capital.

'Nothing can hold that boy back. He's phenomenal, I tell you. He's exactly like his father.'

That night the Portuguese girl didn't show up for dinner. We waited for her until ten in the deserted dining room, and when she didn't come, we went up to our room. The coffee kept me from sleeping, and I heard Juan twisting and turning for a long time. In the middle of the night I woke again with a start and saw his shadow outlined against the window. Outside, somebody was strumming a guitar, and a chorus of voices was softly singing a sweet, melancholy ballad.

I got up on tiptoes to look. The light of the moon peeked faintly through the clouds, and I could distinguish a group of young men singing under the Portuguese girl's balcony. María was wearing a white nightgown with lace edging, and she listened to the ballad without moving. When the boys finished, they saluted her in pantomime, and she leaned over the railing and threw them a kiss.

In the morning I thought I had dreamed it, but Señor

Joaquín winked an eye while serving breakfast and asked if the serenade had kept us awake.

'Not at all,' I said.

'It was my son's idea,' he said. 'It was María's nineteenth birthday yesterday. He brought the guitar and the musicians.'

The sun glared over the leaden sea, but the horizon was still foggy and the wind was still blowing from the land side. The country vacationers were wading at the end of the pier, and a baby with a beach bonnet and long curls was playing on the hotel dock under the watchful eye of his nurse. Across from the fish-shop there were a dozen boats tied to buoys. The manager was weighing boxes with a steelyard. A group of men were watching the operation in silence.

Isabelo was watching too, his hands buried in his pockets. He said that the fishermen came from San Javier and had caught about a hundred twenty-five pounds of mullet in just one casting.

'Why don't they sell them in their own town?' Juan asked.

'They pay better here.'

On the boardwalk the old men were securing weights to the nets, and Isabelo took us to the docks and introduced us to his brother-in-law. Their boat was just a few yards away. While he worked his lighter, he said that until a few months before they had used sails, but that since he had bought an engine they had stripped its masts.

'We're much better off this way,' he concluded.

We had sat down near the hatch of the boat, and the noise of the piston drowned out our words. The smokestack vomited gusts of dirty smoke. Isabelo secured the tiller, and we headed into the wind in the direction of San Javier.

The brother-in-law was smoking in the bow, his beret pushed back, and I looked at the foamy wake opening behind us like a newly plowed furrow. Minutes later the wind began to die down. The boat pitched slightly, and Isabelo swung the tiller. He told us that at dawn they had let down the gill net, but the current was strong and it carried the giltheads away.

Juan got up and sat down next to him, and suddenly he asked him if he had taken part in the serenade in María's honor.

'Me?' Isabelo looked at him as if he were talking nonsense.

'Last night a group of young men serenaded her. Didn't you hear it?'

'Sure, I heard it.' He explained in a hoarse voice that the Portuguese girl enjoyed arousing the boys of the town, and they all ran after her like fools and did whatever she wanted.

'Her father sends her here to punish her, so she won't run around loose ... and she's going back home worse than she came.'

'How about you? Haven't you gone out with her?'

'She tried me out once,' he said, blushing. 'But she won't again.'

'Why?'

'She thought she was going to play with me too, but I taught her a lesson. If you say you're a man, then you've got to play the part come what may. With me, they've got to deliver. I'm no kid.'

The brother-in-law kept watch at the bow and signalled to change course to starboard. We had arrived at a place where the nets had been spread out, and the cork floats of the gill nets bobbed on the surface of the water. Isabelo turned off the engine. When the boat stopped, the brother-in-law pulled the first cork float in, then, rowing slowly with one oar, began to draw in the nets.

Dozens of giltheads were enmeshed in the nets, and as he hauled, Isabelo took them out of the net and threw them on board. Juan watched the spectacle, fascinated. The fish flapped about, agile and brilliant. The brother-in-law let the net out carefully, so that the cork floats and weights wouldn't tangle; when the net was all out of the boat, he gave the oar to Isabelo, and lowered the net little by little until it disappeared.

They started the engine up again. We were running with the wind at our bow now, bearing in the direction we had come. Isabelo took a knife out of his pocket and began to open the giltheads. He would cut out their innards and, once clean, throw them into a tin pail. When he finished, his hands were red, and blood stained the water in the pail. Then he threw the water overboard and washed the deck; the water disappeared down the scupper holes.

'A small catch,' he said as he dried his hands. 'Let's see if we can do better this afternoon.'

'You're going out again?'

'Yes, sir. During the summer we draw the nets twice.'

Isabelo accepted a cigarette Juan offered and laughed, showing all his teeth. 'And the missus? Was she bored?'

'Not at all. I've enjoyed it.'

'This is always the same. If you've seen it once . . . If we go out for mullet, I'll let you know.'

On the boardwalk going back to the hotel, Juan said Isabelo had a fine physique and should attract women once he'd shaved and dressed. He looked at me out of the corner of one eye, and by the way he spoke I realized that he was jealous of Isabelo's virility.

'I don't know, I haven't noticed,' I said.

Someone had leaned his bicycle against the wall of the hotel. I saw the son's sailor hat hanging on the hatstand. The owner asked about our excursion and complained about the bad weather. 'I've never seen such a wind in my life. It will clear up tonight or my name isn't Joaquín.'

Before serving our food, he invited us to taste his Jumilla. He filled two glasses to the brim and asked if we knew French.

'A little,' said Juan.

'I've received a postcard from a guest who was here at the beginning of the summer. An industrialist from Toulouse, a certain M'sieu Lelon . . .I – uh – to tell the truth, I'm not very good at languages.'

He showed Juan the card, a bright-colored one with a view of the city. The text was brief. Juan explained that the Frenchman sent many greetings and hoped to visit him next year.

'They all write the same thing,' exclaimed Señor Joaquín happily. 'It's either the peace they find here or the climate or what have you, but it never fails. Anyone who sets foot in this town always comes back.'

He put the postcard away carefully and leaned on the bar facing us.

'I like to collect postcards. This is the first one I've received from France.'

'I thought a lot of French people came here,' said Juan.

'No, it's Germans, Danes, Scandinavians who come mostly. . . .' He shrugged his shoulders, as if the effort of enumerating them all had worn him out. 'In short, people from all over the world. All except the French.'

There was a pause. Juan said the Jumilla tasted good. Señor Joaquín swelled up with pride.

'In our province there are lots of phenomenal wines,

one for every taste. Just like this town. Here you can fish, go walking, see the countryside. There's something for everyone.'

The Portuguese girl arrived right in the middle of the meal, a towel on her head. She had washed and perfumed her hair with cologne, and she asked Señor Joaquín if he had any news from her parents.

'No, nothing for you.'

María looked at him angrily. Her dark eyes flashed. For a moment I thought she was going to scream, but she dropped into a chair without so much as a sigh.

'What are they waiting for? Do they want me to rot forever in this damn town?'

'Be patient, my girl.' Señor Joaquín came over and gave her an affectionate tap on the shoulder. 'They said they'd be here by the middle of the month. They can't be much longer.'

'If they don't come soon, I'm going to take off. I'm sick of waiting for them. Sick of it.'

'Don't be foolish now.' In Señor Joaquín's solicitude there was a hint of lust. 'What would you do alone in some other place? You wait for them here and then go home with them.'

'I've been here more than two months. I want to get back to the city.'

'You'll go back, girl, you will.'

'I'm young,' she moaned. 'I want to enjoy life.'

'Go ahead, who's stopping you?'

'Here?' She looked at the deserted dining room, the line of chairs in the corner. 'What do you expect me to do here?'

'I don't know; go out, fish, walk with the boys. . . .'

'Oh, shut up,' she said. 'Leave me alone.'

The rest of the meal was eaten in silence. The girl

looked at the street obstinately, as if in ambush for something unforeseen. Señor Joaquín came and went busily. When we went up to our room, Juan said that the girl seemed sincerely sad and her desperation was not feigned.

'You ought to go console her,' I said.

He smiled and threw himself on the bed. Before I fell asleep, I saw him lying there, his arms crossed under his neck, staring up, blowing smoke rings.

When I woke up an hour later, the wind was still blowing. The sea had covered the strip of beach by the pier and was lapping monotonously. Juan was wetting his head under the faucet, and he suggested that we go out in the car. His briefcase filled with projects lay on the bed, and the floor was seeded with cigarette butts. I said yes.

There was no one in the lobby. Some one had taken the bicycle away. Juan got in the car and cleaned the windshield. The town was asleep as usual; the summer homes stood in a row, empty and closed. Zigzagging to avoid the ruts, we reached the main highway and turned toward Cartagena.

Past the sheds at the airbase there is an open field of ocher earth, perpetually parched by the wind. The palm trees wave their plucked plumes ceaselessly; scattered among the windmills you can see farmhouses, yellowing dwarf fig trees, and donkeys with blinkered eyes turning the draw-well. A pair of Civil Guards, their muskets slanted across their backs, pedalled ahead of us. When we passed them they stopped, and I saw them unbutton the chin straps of their tricorns and wipe the sweat from their foreheads.

Half a mile beyond Torre del Negro, Juan stopped the car on the edge of the ditch and made a sign for me to get out.

'Look!' he exclaimed.

A young man in sailor's uniform was bicycling toward a small olive grove. Seated on the handlebar was a tanned girl wearing a blue sweater. After a few seconds – their backs were still to us – he cut off obliquely along a bridle path, and the two disappeared from sight, as if the earth had swallowed them up.

'Do you think it's them?' I said.

'Who knows?' answered Juan. 'Maybe they're lovers.'

On our way to Cabo de Palos we discussed the pros and cons. Juan maintained that María was just acting like a woman, and I took the opposite view. The highway cut through the valley like a knife. Prickly pear trees, agaves, eucalyptuses mingled their different tones of green. In San Gines de la Jara we stopped to photograph a colonial-style hacienda whose palm trees were loaded with dates; it had inviting bay windows and dazzling white walls. Cabo de Palos appeared suddenly behind a wall of dry stones, and while Juan went to survey the vista from the lighthouse, I ambled through the town and sat at a hut in front of the salt wharf and drank a bottle of beer. The warehousemen were still working despite the late hour, and with inexplicable uneasiness, I looked at their straw hats, their dark bodies, their dirty, torn pants. I didn't know why, but I felt terribly alone. I thought of Jaime and our friends and felt like crying.

When Juan returned, the sun had lost its balance and was sliding down behind the tin roofs of the eating stands. The owner came over to take our order. Juan ordered another beer and said that the view from the lagoon was magnificent.

'There are white, sandy beaches miles long. You can sunbathe in the nude.'

He announced that as soon as the weather cleared we'd

go visit the inlet. I tried to smile, without success, and he asked what was the matter with me.

'I've walked a lot,' I said. 'If I lie down a while I'll feel better.'

We returned to town. A strong wind swept the countryside near Algar, and the windmills creaked as they turned. Toward the sea the sky was leaden gray. As he drove, Juan looked at me with concern, and I put a hand around his neck and caressed his cheek.

'Darling,' I said, 'my darling.'

In a few minutes my fatigue disappeared. The plain was shaking off its afternoon torpor. It was almost twilight; there were men and women riding donkeys on the road on their way home from work in the fields. Clouds of dust still hung over Los Urrutias, and here and there Civil Guards stood watch on the shoulder of the road, their hands resting on the stocks of their carbines.

Juan parked next to the bar where María played dominoes with the fishermen. He didn't find her, and we followed the street to the hotel. The sailor's cap was hanging on the hatstand again. Señor Joaquín greeted us affably and asked about our outing.

'We were around Cabo de Palos,' said Juan.

'Did you like it?'

'The view is splendid.'

'Its only good feature, sir,' Señor Joaquín emphasized this with a nod. 'View and all, I still wouldn't set foot in the place.'

'No?'

'No, sir. I'm not out to praise our town, but people there aren't noble like our people are. Here, if anyone has something against you, they say it to your face. Not there; they're all smiles and chitchat, but if you're not careful, they'll strip you of your very skin. They're rascals, believe me.'

We left him blathering on against people in Palos and went to our room to rest. Juan woke me at dinner time. The menu was the same as on the previous days, and I ate but did not enjoy the dried fish, the eggs drowned in oil, the edam cheese and biscuits. Juan drank a whole pitcher of Jumilla without help from me. We stayed there a long time, but María didn't show up. When he took away the dishes Señor Joaquín said she was indisposed.

I had to take a pill in order to sleep that night. I got up late and saw that Juan had already gone out. The floor was covered with cigarette butts, and the briefcase was still on the table – just as he had left it yesterday before our outing.

The weather hadn't changed. Little woolly clouds were sailing west. The tide was out, and the dead sea gleamed; the seagulls seemed suspended in the air, and from time to time descended in curious dives in search of fish.

I found Juan in the dining room, and he told me that Señor Joaquín's son had returned to Cartagena on his bicycle at the break of dawn.

'How do you know?' I said. 'Did you see him?'

'No,' he answered. 'I was still sleeping. .... His father just told me.'

Again we lost ourselves in a sea of intrigues and conjectures. Who was right? The girl? Señor Joaquín? Isabelo? At eleven, Isabelo's brother-in-law came to let us know they were going out for mullet, and I said to Juan that I still didn't feel rested and asked him to go alone. In the restaurant I had bought a dozen postcards with views of the town, and I wrote a few lines to all my friends. I saved the last one for Jaime, but after I wrote his address, I tore it up.

On the way back from the post office, I went swimming from the floats with the country vacationers and nurses. María arrived a little later in a bikini and a blue rubber bathing cap. Greeting me with an offhanded gesture, she ran into the water until she was beyond her depth, and then swam away energetically.

The sun streaked the leaden sea with bands of light, and its reflections hurt my eyes. I swam a few minutes and lay on the wooden slats of the float. María was still swimming out toward the islands. Half an hour later, she came and sat down alongside me and asked about Juan.

'What about your husband? Isn't he bathing?'

I told her he'd gone fishing with Isabelo, and she sighed. 'It's a miserable town, with nothing to do. By ten at night there isn't a soul at the café.'

'Have you been able to talk to your family?'

María took out a Bisonte from her beach bag and lit it with a tiny lighter. 'I'm going to phone them this afternoon. If they don't come for me immediately, I'm leaving on my own.'

There were two fishermen standing on the edge of the pier looking at us, out of the corner of their eye. María shook the ash from her cigarette angrily.

'It's a backward country. The men look at the women as if they were dogs. As soon as I can do as I please, I'll never come back.'

Juan returned very late, his body covered with salt. Isabelo had given him a fish, and he explained that the sea had been rough and the waves had wet the deck. 'Let's hope this damned weather clears up!' he exclaimed. 'I'm dying to go out to the weirs.'

At siesta time I told him about my conversation with María. Juan said that Isabelo had also talked about her, but he couldn't get anything new out of him about her

boat jaunt. In the middle of the afternoon the girl had a
spat with Señor Joaquín. We heard her yelling in the
dining room, and immediately after she shut herself up
in her room, slamming the door, and didn't come out
until supper.

That night there were endless comings and goings in
the hall. Juan slept soundly because of the pills, and in
my half-sleep I seemed to hear the Portuguese girl turning her room upside down, going to the window and
arguing with a man in a loud voice. In the morning Señor
Joaquín looked pale, there were rings under his eyes, and
he didn't recite his usual litany about the weather. While
he served us coffee, he said that María was sick, and they
had taken her at dawn to Cartagena to the clinic of some
friends.

'What's the matter?' said Juan. 'Anything serious?'

'We don't know exactly yet,' said Señor Joaquín, avert-
ing his eyes. 'Maybe it's appendicitis.'

During the following days, María's sudden departure
became our favorite topic. Some maintained that she had
attempted suicide; others that they had it on good
authority that her illness was fatal; and still others insisted that she had fled with a rich foreigner; and em-
broidered their account with all sorts of contradictory
and fantastic details.

Only Señor Joaquín contemptuously dismissed all these
rumors. Every day he would inform us that María was
getting along well, and assured us that in a short time we
would have her back with us. Life at the hotel went on
no differently. One morning, however, the owner received
a lightning visit from his son. When we got up that day we
saw his bicycle leaning against the hotel and his cap on
the hatstand. The two of them shut themselves up in
the kitchen to talk. By lunch time the bicycle and the

cap had disappeared, and Señor Joaquín told us that the patient had almost recovered and would soon be up.

'Poor girl,' he added, 'her parents will be happy to see her.'

There were variable skies all week, with gusts of wind and dark, shapeless, fleeting clouds. The last vacationers from the country closed their homes; I swam alone among the empty floats. Señor Joaquín watched the sea from his wicker armchair. The weather continued to confound his prognostications, and he took it like a personal defeat for which he was fully responsible. Once in a while he'd forget his old boasts about the flood of tourists and dust off reminiscences of a German couple who had stopped at his place six years ago or of a Danish gentleman who had promised to come back with his family and had sent him Christmas greetings. The menu was the same as usual, and after my first rebellious feelings passed, I got used to it little by little.

Juan's briefcase still lay undisturbed on top of the table. Every day I would formulate speeches to him about it in my mind, but when the moment came to speak I would allow the opportunity to pass like a coward and put it off to the following day. Juan went out often with Isabelo and his brother-in-law, and one afternoon I accompanied them while they put out the cane *pasantana*. It was a new way of fishing for me. While the hoop of the net closed, the mullet tried to leap out over the bolt-rope and fell instead into the cane frame previously readied. That time they caught more than two boxes full, and on the way back Isabelo talked about the conditions at Mar Menor. The weirs, he said, had been leased by the state to a group who employed many watchmen and guards. Fishermen were forbidden access to the best spots, and only one day a year, as a special privilege, could they come to these channels, and even then they had to go halves on the catch with the Association.

'What day is that?'

'The twentieth of this month. But if you want to go out to the sandbar before then, I'm free early tomorrow and I'll go with you.'

The brother-in-law wanted to know if we had tasted the local *caldero*. Juan said no.

'It's rice, fisherman style. If you like, we'll take fish with us and prepare it there.'

Juan consulted me with a glance. I looked away, but he answered that he was for it. 'Let's hope it's a good day,' he sighed.

When we got back, Señor Joaquín told us that there had been two phone calls from Barcelona for us.

'Who was it?' I asked. My heart pounded.

'I don't know. A man. He didn't leave a message.'

'Did he want to talk to me?'

'To both of you. To you and then to the gentleman. He'll call later.'

'So long as it isn't bad news,' I said as we went up to our room.

'If it were bad news, we'd already have heard,' Juan replied. 'You won't help things by being nervous. Come on, sit down and stop thinking about it.'

It was the only reasonable thing to do, and for an hour I read a hundred pages or so of a book without understanding anything I read. My attention wandered as I read the words. During dinner the telephone rang again. Señor Joaquín picked it up and gestured to us to come.

'Barcelona. It's for you.'

He handed me the antique phone with a mouthpiece

and a crank, and Jaime's voice came over the receiver.

'Marta, is that you?'

'How did you get our address?'

'Very simple. Gloria got a postcard from that town and I asked for the hotel. . . . Asun and I want to come and see you.'

'That's silly. We're about to leave. We're all ready to go.'

'Then we'll meet on the road. Are you enjoying yourselves?'

'Very much.'

'Can't you talk?'

'No.'

'Is there someone there?'

'We'll see each other in Barcelona. I'll call Asun as soon as we get back.'

Juan had gotten up from the table and he asked, 'Is it Jaime?'

'Yes.'

'What did you say?'

'No, I was talking to Juan.'

'Let me talk.' He took the phone from me and said, 'Jaime?' Jaime's voice over the receiver sounded ridiculous and impotent. 'No, on the contrary, I think it's a magnificent idea. We were beginning to get bored all by ourselves.'

He explained that if they stopped overnight in Valencia they could arrive in time for dinner in two days without getting too worn out.

'The road is good. Tell Asun that we'll be waiting for you. . . . Wait, let me give you Marta again.'

He handed me the phone with a smile.

'You see? Everything's arranged,' said Jaime. 'Are you happy?'

'No.'

'Then what's the matter with you?'

'Nothing. I'd like to get back to Barcelona and work. I'm fed up with travelling.'

'All right, all right, don't be like that. We'll talk later.'

'Good-bye.'

'See you in two days.'

Señor Joaquín hadn't missed a word of the conversation. As we were returning to the table he wanted to know how many friends were coming and explained that he could kill a chicken and sauté it Murcia-style.

'Do what you think best,' I said.

Juan was placidly drinking the Jumilla in the pitcher and looked at me disapprovingly.

'Jaime likes that very much.'

'I hope he enjoys it. He doesn't have to come all the way here to eat it.'

'I thought you were getting bored all alone. That's why I invited them.'

'I don't want to see anyone,' I answered.

The next day we went to the weirs, and I got over my bad humor. The blue sea rippled smoothly, and for the first time you couldn't see a cloud in the whole sky. Isabelo was waiting on the pier, clean-shaven and wearing a new shirt. His brother-in-law had gone to Elche to see the Real Madrid soccer team play, and Juan helped me jump on board. Below deck there was a basket with bottles of wine, dishes and napkins, and a black cauldron in a basket holder. Isabelo untied the boat and turned on the engine. Little by little the houses of the town got smaller. The boat didn't pitch at all, and as we went along the islands and the lighthouse and the sinuous profile of the sandbar stood out more clearly.

Isabelo had sat down in the stern near the tiller, and I

made myself comfortable on the canvas that covered the wicker frame of the *pasantana* and gazed at the wake. The sun shining on the sea made it look like oilcloth. You could see schools of tiny fish in the clear water swimming toward the coast in search of warmth, and when we reached the deep water the bow created rippling waves on the surface. 'Good weather at last!' exclaimed Juan.

Half an hour later, we were moving along the coast again and Isabelo secured the tiller. The wide beach looked parched and white in the distance. A black buoy served as a marker of the concession's limits for the fishermen. When the engine stopped, there was an unbroken calm on the surface of the water. Isabelo looked toward the float of the Association and said there were visitors at the chalet.

'What chalet?'

'That building you see back of us. It's a recreation pavilion for the administrators.'

He went forward, using the oar as a paddle in order not to get stuck on the sand banks, and when we reached shore, he threw out the anchor and we jumped out.

'You can go swimming in peace here,' he said.

It looked as if the beach had no end. The sun shone from straight overhead, and not a breath of wind was blowing. Straight ahead of us Cabezo Gordo dissolved in the haze on the horizon.

We took off our clothes. The sandbar fishermen had built a kind of refuge to weave and dye the nets. Near the edge of the floats I could see the remains of various cooking fires and recent signs of visitors. Isabelo showed us the barrels of dye. He had brought the basket from the boat and Juan insisted on opening a bottle of Jumilla. Isabelo also drank happily, and the three of us went off across the dunes to look at the weir.

The first fishing weir had a width of approximately thirty yards. On both shores there was a small wall to channel the current, and we followed it alongside the sleepy, clear water. On the other side, on a small island formed by the two arms of the inlet was the recreation pavilion of the Association, a two-storey building with a slightly run-down look and a wide balcony looking out toward the sea. There was a yacht tied to the pier, and visitors were dancing on the terrace of the chalet to music from a record player. As we got closer to the weir I recognized the melody of *Negra Consentida*. In the lonely silence of the lagoon the music sounded strange. The couples rocked smoothly cheek to cheek, and two girls dressed in white lace were doing turns too, looking as exquisite and fragile as porcelain figures.

'Later they eat and go lie down wherever they want,' said Isabelo. 'These people certainly know how to enjoy life.'

The record player suddenly started playing a foxtrot of the forties, and we continued along the upper edge of the small wall until we reached the weir. A barrier of cane cut the cove in two, and by means of a complicated system of nets, the fish which came from Mar Menor, attracted by fresh currents, would head into a series of corrals from which they could not get out. A short while after we arrived, a man in a smooth-bottom boat headed for the first weir. After closing the mouth entrance, he jumped inside and with a hand net began to transfer the fish to a pail.

The outer shore of the sandbar was also magnificent. The beach went on for miles and miles. To the right of the lighthouse, a pilot's boat sat athwart the horizon. The ground was covered with seaweed and rushes. Crab apple trees climbed up over the dunes, and I found a snake's shed skin intact. Isabelo walked ahead, looking for wood to burn.

When we got back to the refuge, Juan opened a bottle of Jumilla and drank half of it in one swig. With four rocks Isabelo improvised a bed for the fire and the cauldron. In the basket there was a platter with mullet and crawfish and a special mortar for the sauce. While I crushed the garlic cloves and hot peppers, Isabelo took out his knife and cut up a hemp rope. Then he added the fish and sauce to the water in the cauldron and set fire to the rope with his lighter.

Juan and I sat down on some beams to watch him. The sweat ran down his forehead, and he took off his shirt and exposed a dark, hairy chest. Juan would now and then pass him the wine, and when he finished one bottle, he uncorked another and offered it to me. 'Go on, drink. We've got to get drunk.'

I obeyed him, and Isabelo accepted with a smile and drank too. After a while, Isabelo took the cauldron off the fire, drained off the juice, and emptied the fish into an earthenware crock. He immediately put the contents of a package of rice in the sauce and, handling the cauldron with its basket cover to keep from burning his hands, again hung the cauldron from the tripod.

It was past three when we were ready to eat. The top of the hatch served as a table, and Isabelo served the fish and rice. Juan said he'd never had a better dish in his life. It also seemed excellent to me, and Isabelo laughed at our enthusiasm. The sauce stung our mouths and the wine disappeared quickly. Juan uncorked the last bottle before dessert and drank from it for a long time, until the wine ran down his chin and stained his bathing suit. Unexpectedly, he stopped and handed it to Isabelo.

'Now that no one can hear you, tell us about your run-in with María,' he said in a hoarse voice.

Isabelo arched his heavy eyebrows and smiled in a forced way.

'There's nothing to tell. She rented the boat just as you do, and one day we came here to the sandbar and quarrelled.'

'Your brother-in-law said that she threw herself at you and used to go looking for you at the town bar every night,' insisted Juan.

'The girl is used to life in the city, to going out in a group with others, and she was bored here. That's why she would run after someone one day, another the next, and then again another on the third. She just didn't know that such things don't go well in a small town.'

'And you? What did you do with her?'

'Nothing.' Isabelo looked away and stared at the ground. 'What men and women do when they're alone.'

A gust of wind shook the stagnant surface of the sea. The guests at the recreation pavilion had gathered at the dock and started to board the yacht. Juan watched me with wine-reddened eyes. Suddenly, he got up, still holding the bottle, faced Isabelo, and said he was taking a walk along the sandbar.

'I leave my wife in your care,' he added, smiling.

My eyes followed him as he stumbled and raised his elbow to drink from the bottle. I felt like running after him and slapping his face. Isabelo, at my side, seemed as confounded as I was.

'Forgive me,' I said. 'He's drunk too much.'

'I should have thought of it before. New wine is very treacherous. Do you want me to keep an eye on him?'

'Thanks, it's not necessary. When he's gotten over it, he'll come back.'

'I meant he shouldn't let the sun shine on his bare head. I have a straw hat on board.'

'Don't worry, he's used to it.' My cheeks burned and I stood up. 'It's not the first time this has happened.'

The water near the shore was calm, and I swam for a few minutes without getting far from shore. The seagulls flew over the grass on the shoal. The Association's yacht had upped anchor and was sailing toward San Javier. When I got out of the water, Isabelo was scrubbing the plates and the inside of the cauldron with sand and straw. As soon as everything was tidy, he rolled up his pants and plunged into the water. I drew my robe around me and contemplated the empty scene, the calm water, the motionless rushes. The early evening light impregnated the air with a diffused phosphorescence. Isabelo kept on swimming. I knew that Juan was crying in some hiding place on the sandbar, and I felt as if I were trapped in a net.

Juan showed up an hour later, calm and serene, with that same vague smile I had first seen the day he asked me for the letters. He explained that he had walked several miles on the dunes, found a post of the Civil Guard, and stopped to chat.

'The sergeant is a fantastic Galician,' he said. 'He was at the Smolensk front, and he's still dreaming of attacking Russians. And you two? What kind of time did you have?'

'Fine,' I answered.

It was getting dark and we went back to the boat. Clouds were gathering again toward the north, and we had the wind at our backs as we went home. During the whole trip none of us said a word. Isabelo stretched out on the canvas covering the nets and watched the tiller. I sat on top of the hatch and smoked. Juan sat at the bow and absently watched the horizon.

In the hotel, Señor Joaquín was waiting for us as if we were rain in May. He had received a telegram from María's parents saying they would arrive the next day, and he was bubbling over with good feeling and bustling about.

'Things are really hot, yes sir. If your friends should take it into their heads to bring others, I'll have to sleep out on the street. I tell you, this town gets more than its share of people.'

That night Juan remained obstinately silent, and I heard him toss and turn in bed. At last he reached for the light switch and went to the chest of drawers for sleeping pills.

'Darling,' I said.

He turned to look at me, and the orphaned, helpless expression on his face made me cry.

'Why did you leave us on the sandbar? Did you think I was going to sleep with him?'

'I don't know.' He moved his lips as if he were going to add something, but he said nothing.

'I don't love Isabelo or anyone else, you understand? I only love you.'

'Yes.'

'You torture yourself pointlessly, do you know that? You're embittering your own life and mine.'

He sat down on the edge of the bed, and I brought his face close to mine until my tears ran down his cheeks.

'You can't go on this way, my darling. You must work, you must be in touch with things. You're just going to pieces here little by little. . . .'

Juan kept saying yes like a child, and when I put out

the light, he lay down at my side and we slept in each other's arms until well into the morning.

Jaime and Asun arrived at one in the afternoon, full of laughter and excitement. They broke into our room, escorted by Señor Joaquín, and Asun kissed me on both cheeks as Jaime leaned over Juan and clapped him affectionately on the back.

'How are you, you rascal? Aren't you ashamed to be getting up at this hour?'

He kissed me too and said that in Barcelona everyone was angry with us and making some very severe judgments about our behavior.

'I bet you wouldn't even know what places to go to now. If you were looking for one of the gang at night, where would you go?'

'To Panams,' I said.

'You see!' he exclaimed triumphantly. 'You're not up on things! You're as out of fashion as open-air dance halls and filter-tip cigarettes. Now we smoke Philippine tobacco and meet at the Jamboree.'

Juan got up, naked to the waist, and looked at Jaime, squinting as if he had forgotten how Jaime looked and was trying quickly to engrave his image anew in his mind.

'Marta was beginning to get bored,' he said. 'That's why I asked you to come.'

'It's not true,' I protested. 'I'll be damned if I wanted to see anyone. . . . I was taking the solitary cure and you've forced me to break my diet.'

'This place is worse than Africa,' said Asun. 'The town looks completely deserted. Has there been an earthquake or something?'

'It's always like this,' I said.

'You two are going to end up in a convent, I swear.' Asun moved close to Juan and shook a finger at him. 'You can't imagine how lively it was in Tossa. More than ten bars opened this summer. We went to bed at four every night.'

'You did?' said Juan. 'May I ask what you were doing?'

'Dancing the Pachanga, drinking daiquiris. . . . On Saturdays and Sundays, the atmosphere's absolutely fantastic. The beach gets jammed with people from Barcelona, and Andalusian workers go around seducing foreigners.'

While they were taking their bags to their rooms, I washed my face and dressed. Juan lathered to shave and seemed to be in a fine mood. Before going downstairs, I went over to him and put my head on his shoulder.

'I'm in love with you, you hear? Promise me you won't drink or do anything foolish.'

Asun came to get me a few moments later. In the lobby Señor Joaquín was talking animatedly to Jaime and insisting that he park his car by the hotel.

'It will be safer there, believe me. Park it next to your friends' and there'll still be space enough for those Portuguese I was telling you about.'

Jaime couldn't get out of it and went through the manoeuvre with the owner looking on complacently. Then he went up to talk to Juan while Asun and I strolled on the pier. At lunch, the four of us met in front of the dock. There was an Austin with a Porto license plate on the street, and Señor Joaquín, acting like a master of ceremonies, introduced us to María's parents. He said she had completely recovered, and they were going to pick her up at the clinic that afternoon. We finally managed to get to the dining room, and a girl in a white apron served us appetizers and chicken à la Murciana.

'What plans do you have for tonight?' asked Asun when we finished.

'None,' said Juan. 'If the town bores you, we can take a drive to Cartagena.'

That's what we decided to do – despite Señor Joaquín's assurances that the people there were not noble like those in his town, nor nice to visitors.

'The Cartagenians have long fingers, gentlemen. Be careful or they'll swipe your wallets.'

We had coffee at the fishermen's bar, and at sunset we got ready to go. Asun wanted all four of us to go in one car, but Juan protested and said he preferred to go alone with her.

'Marta and I have been in each other's company too long. It's good to change sometimes, don't you agree?'

They both laughed and got into the Seat. Jaime opened the door of the car and we took off after them immediately.

'Will you tell me what's the matter with you?' he said when we were out of town.

He had turned to look at me, his hand resting on the gearshift, but I didn't move.

'Nothing,' I answered. 'I didn't want you to come. I'm tired, Jaime.'

'Tired? Of what?'

'Everything. Of the way we all live, Barcelona, our friends. . . .'

The red and white markers on the old airfield peeked out of the weeds. Farther on, the countryside was blurred by a thick cloud of dust.

'I've been thinking a lot lately, and I see things clearly now. We were both fooling ourselves this spring. . . . I'm in love with Juan.'

'You've always been in love with Juan.'

'I know that, but I didn't realize it then. I didn't know

how much he loved me. When I told him about us –'

'What?'

'Please, don't let go of the wheel.'

'What did you say?'

'Watch where you're driving,' I said. 'We'll have an accident.'

'Were you really capable of . . .'

'I had already stopped giving it any importance and I was almost joking when I told him.'

Jaime kept driving, his face tense, then he suddenly accelerated. 'What right did you have to tell him a secret that wasn't yours?'

'You know me well enough, Jaime. I've never wanted to be disloyal.'

'But you *are* disloyal. The secret was as much mine as yours. How am I going to act when I see him?'

'Don't yell like that, please.'

'If I want to yell, I'll yell. Do you hear?'

'I'm not deaf.'

We were getting near Algar, and I watched the triangular arms of the windmills. Jaime was hunched over the wheel. A cyclist crossed the road without warning, but Jaime's reflexes were good and he quickly swerved around him.

'Tell me, what kind of an act can I put on?'

'None. It's an affair between him and me. No one's calling you to account.'

'Shut up, for God's sake. At least shut up.'

Near La Union the road widened. We went through the town fast, and on the other side of it we saw the Seat again. The setting sun lighted the mounds of slag and the ruins of the foundry chimneys. To the right the lights of a factory could be seen. A jeep with an American license plate turned onto the road to Escombreras, and after a level crossing Juan stopped and yelled through the car window for us to follow.

We circled the city by a road below the city wall, and the atmosphere of the port delighted me. Men from the naval squadron in dress uniforms circulated in groups, and there were also many soldiers and marines. Juan parked in the town plaza. For a few minutes we filed down a street filled with people. At the other end of it, the captain's guard was lowering the colors, and traffic stopped while they stood at attention. When the ceremony was over, we asked the way to El Molinete, and we climbed a narrow, steep street to the upper town.

There was a badly lit plaza up there, and it seemed as if every draftee had a date. Some women were waiting around, hugging their purses under their arms. The men formed a circle around them and also looked us up and down. In the bars, the loudspeakers were turned up to full volume. After much hesitation, we decided on one, and Juan ordered four cuba libres.

'I'm ashamed,' murmured Asun, pointing to the waitresses. 'What must they think of us?'

'Act as if you're a professional. Look at Marta. No one would think she's married.' Juan turned to Jaime and asked him, 'Isn't that so?'

Jaime attempted to smile apologetically. Asun had gone up close to him and hung on his arm.

'I'd like to dance,' I said.

'I saw a dance hall for sailors before we passed the plaza.'

'Where?'

'I don't remember.' Asun took the cuba libre and raised it to her lips. 'I'm going to drink to get in shape.'

'I'm in shape already,' I said. 'It's my first night on the town in months.'

'What did you do in your town at night?'

'Nothing, sleep. We have to make up for lost time.'

Jaime remained silent. Juan observed him with interest and then looked at me a few seconds.

'You look a little down in the dumps,' he said.

'It's the heat. As soon as I drink a little, I'll get over it.'

'Then drink. Today's a big day.'

'Yes,' added Asun. 'We're together again at last.'

The women at the bar were talking with the customers. Now and then some soldiers came in, looked the place over, and went back to the street immediately.

'I'm thirsty,' I said. 'I'll have another cuba libre.'

'Wait till we get to the sailors' place,' said Asun.

'Let her drink if she wants to.' Juan called the waitress and looked disapprovingly at Jaime's glass which was still full. 'Come on, liven up.'

'I *am* livened up.'

'Please bring us four more,' Juan ordered.

'I want to dance,' I said. 'I've never in my life wanted to dance the way I want to today.'

The waitress put on a new record in the jukebox and poured a jigger of Larios and half a bottle of Coca-Cola into my glass.

'Lemon?'

'A sliver, thanks.'

A character with a face like a monkey's had approached Juan and handed him a piece of paper. The little fellow's shirttails were hanging out. I looked down and saw he was barefoot.

'What does he want?' asked Asun.

'*Can you give any I am deaf and dumb,*' Juan read in English.

'He's a mute,' explained the waitress. 'He thinks you're Americans.' She faced the little man and started to move her fingers agilely. 'They're Spaniards, you jerk. Or are you blind now too?'

The little man looked at us; he didn't understand. Juan gave him five *duros* and he vanished immediately.

'Poor fellow, he earns his beans this way,' said the waitress. 'A few pennies here and there. He's not bad, really, and he leads a dog's life.'

'You should have kept the paper,' said Asun.

'Do you really want it?' The waitress had lit a cigarette, and she put the pack back in her bosom. 'Ginés!' she yelled. 'Go and get Tirao back right away.'

'Please don't bother. I was just talking.'

'It's no bother, miss. He has a whole bunch in several languages. People from everywhere come here. . . .'

A tall, black-haired man who looked like a gypsy and wore the shirt and rope belt of the followers of St Francis stopped arguing with the women and rushed out into the street.

'You're ridiculous,' Jaime said in a low voice. 'Can you tell me why the hell you asked for the card?'

Juan gave him a surprised look. Jaime seemed genuinely furious.

'It's obvious you can't go out anywhere with you without your making some kind of blunder.'

'What in the world's eating you?' Asun turned to me for support. 'What did I do to him? Tell me what did I do? Good lord, right out of the blue!'

'If Asun wants the man's paper,' I said, 'what business is it of yours?'

'It's a goddam pain to watch her put on that ladylike act,' said Jaime. 'It gives me a pain and the whole thing's loathsome.'

'When a character like him passes out cards, it's for people to keep,' Asun protested. 'I was just beginning to enjoy myself and you had to kick up a fuss. God, you must have gotten up on the wrong side of the bed.'

The man returned with the mute. He held him tight and roughly pushed and dragged him toward us.

'Where had you sneaked off to, you bugger?' The waitress leaned over the bar and made a threatening gesture toward him with her arm. 'You think it's nice to scoot off and not say thanks to these people? Come on, give them the card! With ears like yours you can applaud behind your neck, you shit.'

The mute began a series of quick gestures. The tall man's dark hand was still holding his collar.

'He's as good as bread, really,' said the woman. 'When we're alone, my friends and I call for him and ask him to tell us how he came into the world. Or to dance the Cha-Cha-Cha. Or act like a fairy. And, let me tell you, you can bust your sides laughing. . . . Hey, Tirao!' she yelled, blocking his way. 'What was your mother's profession?'

The mute seemed to have caught on, and stretched his mouth wide and showed his gums. His fingers leafed through an imaginary roll of bills. Then he emitted a hoarse sound and began to waggle his hips.

'He's explaining she was a whore.' The waitress began to choke with laughter. 'I told you, didn't I? How about your brothers? Come on, tell us. Where are your brothers?'

The people at the bar formed a ring around us, and the waitress repeated the question and grimaced. The tall man grabbed the mute by his shirttails.

'Your brothers, where are they now?'

Tirao groaned some more. He moved his lips, stuck out his tongue, and rolled his eyes.

'Dead, yes,' said the tall man. 'But where? In the cemetery?'

'They're at the clinic preserved in a bottle of alcohol.' The waitress held her sides. 'Oh, oh, I'll piss from laughing! What a character! You'd think Frankenstein was his father. If you took a photograph of him, he'd break the camera!'

Two military police looked in at the door, both with armbands, clubs, and American helmets. Juan pointed to the empty glasses and offered a round of cuba libres to the woman. The jukebox played a song by the Platters.

'Give the mute one, too.'

'He only drinks soda pop.' The woman took one out of the icebox and opened it. 'Go on, drink. The gentleman's paying.'

Tirao thanked him with a groan. He grabbed the bottle, lifted his elbow, and drank it all in one gulp.

'How about you? Wouldn't you like something?'

'Give me a glass of cazalla, Merche,' said the tall man.

Jaime hadn't stopped frowning. I heard him arguing with Asun in a low voice, and I told Juan I wanted to go dancing. When he paid, we walked out, and we had to open a path among the soldiers watching the comings and goings of the women. The mute and the tall man joined us.

'Are you from out of town?'

'Yes.'

'Madrid?'

'No, Barcelona.'

The man with the rope belt took Juan's arm and told him that Barcelona was the best place in the world.'It's a city with class, am I right? When you go down the Ramblas, you see women there you can't find anywhere else. I was there as a tourist once with some gentlemen, the way you're travelling now, and we had a grand time. Many people from Cartagena go to Barcelona to work, but I've got plenty of work here, I keep telling myself. You have to have dough there. If you've got cash in your wallet, you can get a run for your money and enjoy life.'

The bar's loudspeaker was playing one of Marchena's songs. Several soldiers clapped to it, and as we crossed the plaza, Asun whispered to me, 'Did you notice?'

'What?'

'Jaime is more unbearable than ever. I don't know what he's got against me.'

'Don't pay any attention. He'll calm down.'

'He was the one who insisted on coming down, and now he blames me.'

The dance hall was a run-down place with a very long bar and a stage closed off with a filthy curtain. An American jukebox was playing *El Gato Montés*. Soldiers and sailors were dancing the pasodoble, clutching their women tightly; when the music stopped, they quickly left the floor and lined up along the bar and at the slot machines.

The waitress at the bar served us four cuba libres, one cazalla, and one soda pop. Jaime drank his in one gulp and gave Asun a nasty look. I asked him if he wanted to dance with me and he said no.

'How about you?'

'I don't want to either,' said Juan.

'How dull they are,' said Asun. 'Let's dance with each other.'

The jukebox started playing *España Cañi*, and we went out on the floor among the sailors and soldiers. The pasodoble was perfect for the place. Asun allowed herself to be led docilely, and I saw the mute dancing with a waitress. The tall man stuck close to Juan. As I passed by I heard him say, 'You just say come to Barcelona, and I'd leave with you this very minute.' Asun leaned her cheek against mine and pointed toward Jaime : 'He'll louse up the party, you'll see.'

'You think so?'

'I'm not sure, but I don't like his expression. Did he say anything on the way here?'

'No.'

'He gets irked about the slightest thing lately. If you could only talk to him. . . . I've tried a thousand times, and I assure you it's useless.'

'I'll try,' I said.

We returned to the bar. The tall man had taken out a pencil and was writing down an address. Jaime was drinking another cuba libre. The music started again soon, and a short little soldier came up to Juan.

'With your permission, sir?'

Juan smiled, and I followed the soldier to the center of the floor. Again *El Gato Montés*, and I wanted the record not to end. The young man danced well. He held me firmly by the waist, and now and then his hand wandered, trying out the terrain. Asun was also dancing with a sailor. When the music stopped, she came over to me.

'I've given a handful of coins to the mute to keep the jukebox going,' she said. 'What do you prefer?'

'Pasodobles,' I begged. 'Only pasodobles.'

We went to pick them out, making a path through the onlookers, and for some unknown reason Jaime and Asun had words. They started to argue nastily, and Juan intervened and took Jaime outside.

'Didn't I tell you?' Asun said heatedly. 'He's got it in for me.'

'What happened?'

'Nothing. I wasn't even looking his way, and he began to insult me furiously. Jesus, what a character!'

I said some consoling words, and since the soldier urged me, I again danced *El Gato Montés*. Asun had her sailor as a partner again. The music became wilder with repetition. A fat waitress was making passes with her apron, and the deaf mute would charge like a bull. My partner didn't waste time this turn. His hand travelled nonchalantly over my back, and he brought his face nearer to mine.

'Your friends, have they left?'

'No,' I answered.

'Do you have a date with them?'

'Yes.'

'And tomorrow?'

'Also.'

'I like you, ma'am. I'd like to see you alone.'

'I'm leaving. I don't live here.'

'It's not true. Tell me what day you're free.'

I invented one to get rid of him, and after a few minutes, Juan returned and paid the bill. Asun had gone out to look for Jaime. The four of us walked through the town in silence. The tall man with the rope belt followed us, drunk too, and embraced Juan.

'Juanillo, will you write?'

'Yes.'

'You've got my address. You write yours in your letter and I'll answer.'

'Yes.'

'That way we'll be in touch, and as soon as you show up here, you let me know and we'll go around together.'

'Yes, yes.'

Asun sat down at the wheel of the car and opened the door for Jaime. We got in the Seat, and before he turned on the ignition, Juan said he'd go slow so they wouldn't lose us.

During the return trip we didn't exchange a word. The landscape looked uninhabited. The Civil Guard stopped us near the town, but when they saw on Juan's identification card that he was a lieutenant, they came to attention and begged his pardon. That night we went to sleep immediately.

The next day we got up very late. I went down to the dining room about one, and Señor Joaquín announced sorrowfully that María and her parents had left at dawn and hadn't been able to say good-bye to us.

'And our friends?' I asked.

'They're still in bed.'

I went out to the pier. The sea was gray and still, and the light danced on the water dully. On the hotel dock sat a sailor with a sad, dreamy look, gazing into the distance. The bicycle occupied its usual place against the wall, and I thought about María's mysterious idyll.

Juan appeared a little later, clean and shaven. He took my arm, and we walked arm in arm to the outskirts of the town. Something had changed in his manner, and he seemed happy to be alive.

When we got to the military area, he stopped and handed me the sheaf of Jaime's love letters.

'Keep them,' he said. 'It doesn't matter at all now.'

Fourth

I HADN'T been back since my first appointment abroad. I took a good look through the window of the taxi at the yellow and ocher building, the familiar green of the eucalyptuses, the gigantic mushroom top of the parasol pine. The house had been built toward the end of the century on the foundations of an old farmhouse, and from afar it looked somewhat conventional. A wood of cork trees girdled it, closing it in uphill, and the front windows looked out on garden beds and commanded a view of terraces sloping down like wide stairs to the deep, irregular bed of the waterway. The cab driver honked his horn at each turn, and at one point I was able to spy the house for just a few seconds, looking slightly tilted, behind a thick curtain of prickly pears. Then it disappeared altogether, and once past the curve the car turned into an earth road; with an intensity that surprised me, I remembered the rambling walks, staying up all night, the marvellous excursions in the two-wheeled carriage.

My friendship with Miguel had begun in college. His mother was an energetic, generous woman who loved me as if I were one of her sons. When my father died, she invited me to spend summers with them at Mas, and from that time on I became another member of the family. Doña Luz fixed up a room for me opposite Armando's, and little by little that house – with its ponds, corrals, and corridors – became the backdrop for the dreams that made up my personal mythology. Miguel and I were inseparable, and up until the time I finished school the best times of my life were spent with him. Mas was the head-quarters where we met to drink, talk, argue about itineraries, projects, books. During the summer months, we swam in the pond and sunbathed on the grass. When it got cold, Miguel held gatherings of his friends in front of the dining room fireplace. There I would tell him every week about my adventures with the opposite sex, and it was there that I heard him mention Mara's name for the first time. Mas was an ideal place for talking, and we considered it our very own lair.

Everything suddenly changed when I was twenty-five. I had gotten my master's degree and accepted a post in Oslo to lecture on Spanish literature, then one in Heidelberg, and two in Paris. Miguel's mother died a few months after I had left, and he took over the administration of her business affairs. Later I received a wedding invitation. 'The time has come to settle down,' it said. I wrote him frequently, but after he was married letters from him came less often. Miguel talked ironically about the joys of married life and sent me news of his son's birth. That year the newspapers often mentioned his name because of a prize his book won. Miguel sent me a copy with a personal dedication, but didn't write again after that. The last cards I had sent had not been answered. I planned to spend the summer with Régine at a beach house at Les Graus du Roi, and I had not been thinking of him. When the term was over, Régine's father fell ill, and we agreed that for the first weeks of vacation each of us would take off on his own. The night I took her to the train I felt terribly alone. What had happened to Armando made me think again about Mas and Miguel. As I passed by the post office I went in and sent him a telegram telling him I was coming. Mara answered me the following day with another telegram: *Our only regret*

*is not having seen you frequently enough during your
first thirty years stop we are resolved to repair this
omission in the ones to follow.*

The taxi drove slowly, skirting ruts and ridges, and
after passing the barn and stables, went along the back
of the house and stopped by the garden. The terrace was
deserted, but on the recently swept gravel there were a
great number of lounge chairs, cushions, folding chairs,
and even a tiny plastic swimming pool for the baby. The
driver helped me take out my bags, and I gave him five
hundred-peseta bills. He pretended to look for change,
but I told him he could keep it.

When I left Barcelona, the sky had been cloudy; then
it cleared up again, and now the sun was shining once
more through the branches of the eucalyptuses. Frogs
were croaking in the pond, and I went toward it to see
the view from the summer-house. I knew the scene well,
and it made me happy to learn that I had not forgotten
it. The hills, covered with carobs and grapevines, sloped
gently down toward the coast. The green of the pines
alternated with the yellow of the wheat fields, and farther
on sky and sea merged in an imprecise blue fringe. A
ravine ran down the middle, with a cortege of reeds
and poplars. In the valley, there was still that same
silence – interrupted only by the sound of the angelus
and the monotonous echo of the blows of a woodcutter's
axe.

On the outside, at least, the house had not changed
either. Immortelles still grew between the tiles on the
roof, and swallows nested under the eaves. The vane of
the lightning rod pointed southeast, and I remembered
practising sharpshooting with Miguel when his mother
gave him a shotgun and we dreamt of organizing safaris
in Africa. When I neared the footbridge that led from

the gallery to the vegetable garden, I stopped to breathe in the odor of the grape skins that rose from the vat. Miguel, Armando, and I often stomped on the grapes with the pressers and drank wine from their jugs until we got high. Large grape baskets were piled up in the outside passage of the house, and piles of pressed grapes were fermenting in the sun. I finally noticed that a woman was coming down the path with a basket of fruit. She shaded her eyes with one hand and looked at me.

'Damiana,' I said.

She stammered, looked confused, and finally put the basket down on the balustrade and embraced me.

'Sir . . .'

'What a long time, Damiana. Do you remember?'

Her face was still fresh and young. She was wearing her hair rather short and brushed back, and she had on a rather tight blue blouse. She had always liked to dress well.

'How could I forget!' she said. 'Good heavens!' José's wife looked at me with moist eyes; suddenly her expression changed, and she broke into tears. 'Have you heard about our misfortune?' Without giving me time to answer, she told me what had happened to Armando. 'They came at midnight, sir. We were all in bed and you can't imagine the uproar they started. . . .'

'I know, Damiana, I know about it.'

'Since then there's something on my mind that doesn't let me sleep. At night I just toss and turn. . . . José doesn't know what to do to calm me.'

'How is José?'

'Oh, he's fine. Just now he's out with the cart gathering hay for the cows.'

'And Antonio? He must be almost a man.'

'Oh, wait till you see him!' Damiana dried her tears,

but could not manage to smile yet. 'You won't know him. He's going to be like his father. For two years he's been going to Mossén Pere's school, and he already knows how to read and write.'

A breeze made the tops of the cypresses sway lightly. Bees buzzed, hidden in the eucalyptuses. A large blackbird stood on the ridge of the roof and suddenly flew straight to the cork trees.

'Miss Mara is down at the beach with the baby and Master Jorge. I think they'll be back soon. When I heard the car, I thought it was them.'

'And Miguel?' I said.

'In the morning he always stays here. He can't be far. Did you look in his room?'

'No, not yet.'

'Well, you go look. I'll take the bags, sir.'

'Thanks, Damiana.'

I entered the gallery and felt my heart pound. A record player had replaced the old Telefunken, and record covers littered the sofa and chairs: songs by Marlene Dietrich and Ella Fitzgerald, charlestons by Paul Whiteman, calypsos and javas. On the table were empty Coca-Cola and wine bottles. No one had bothered to empty the ashtrays.

In the library, the bound collection of *La Ilustración Española y Americana* slept behind the glass doors of the bookcase. When I was young, I used to spend whole afternoons looking through them in the garden, and I went over to touch the missal with metal corners that had belonged to Doña Luz. Her solemn portrait was still in the same place, facing her husband's. I examined it a moment – just enough to remember the lines of her face – and then headed down the corridor with rooms on either side.

Miguel's room looked out on the orchards toward the front, and I walked in without knocking. Someone had closed the shutters, but light came in through the cracks. Miguel was not there.

The room still looked like a lion's den. Books were piled up by the dozen on top of the desk – dictionaries, grammars, geological and botanical monographs, philosophical and scientific books. On the arm of the divan there was a cup of coffee and leftovers from a snack.

Damiana had left the bags in my room, and I went to look at it. The room smelled musty, as if it hadn't been lived in for a long time. The furniture was the same as five years ago, and I remembered the religious chromo on the wall, framed in lace and purple shells.

José's wife complained about the dirty condition of the house – she wasn't to blame, she added immediately: it was the new tenant family who lived down below; hiring them had been a hasty decision of Miguel's mother a few months before she died. Since they had arrived, everything was topsy-turvy. Dust accumulated under the beds, and no one thought of lifting the bellglass and winding the clock. She didn't understand how the gentlemen could be so patient.

'Besides, they're very quarrelsome. As soon as they see me, they put on angry faces.'

José's house was some twenty yards from the big house, and I took a turn in the garden with Damiana. In the stables a young man I didn't know was taking the pack-saddle off a chestnut horse full of sores. Since she went by him without greeting him, I decided he must belong to the rival band.

'José will have a pleasant surprise when he sees you. He's always talking about you. This morning he asked Master Miguel when you were arriving.'

The hens pecked in the vegetable garden, and the dogs started barking. Damiana threatened them with a wave of her hand. 'Shut up, imbeciles, don't you see it's Master Bruno?' But they sniffed me suspiciously and barked louder. The smallest was a curly-haired fox-terrier with a short snout, trained no doubt for hunting. I knelt to stroke him, and he immediately let himself be petted and then started jumping and whining excitedly around me.

'José!' yelled Damiana. 'Look who's come!'

I sat on the wall of the vegetable garden and looked at the view of the valley. The workers on the opposite slope were lighting weeds to fertilize the soil. The wind was sweeping the clouds toward the mountain. On the lower terraces, seeds were beginning to sprout.

José came out, hitching up his pants. He had just wet his head – the water was still running down his face – and he squeezed my hand clumsily. 'For goodness' sake!' he kept repeating. 'Who would have thought it!'

He seemed happy to see me, and his face widened in a smile. I too was happy to be with him again after so long a time, and I said that I found him still the same.

'His hair is beginning to fall out,' said Damiana.

José stroked the hair on his chest. 'So long as I don't lose it below.'

'How's hunting?' I asked.

'So-so.' José gestured with one hand. 'I don't know what's happening to the rabbits, but there are fewer each time I go out. Last year, on the other hand, there was plenty of partridge. Miguel and I got more than three hundred.'

The dogs surrounded him, whining and rubbing themselves against his pants legs.

'Aside from that,' I said, 'how are things with you?'

'Here, it's always the same. ... Spring, summer, autumn, winter, and then all over again.'

'Are you doing well?'

'It's rained a lot this year.'

Damiana broke in to say that without the other tenants things would be much better.

'Keep quiet, woman,' said José. 'Why should he care?'

I had given him my pack of cigarettes, and he gave me a light with his lighter. 'You've already heard about Armando?'

'Yes.'

'I'd been afraid it would happen,' he said. 'God damn!'

Antonio appeared in the window. He had opened his mouth to say something and, when he saw me, remained quiet.

'Come on,' said Damiana. 'Don't you know this gentleman?'

The boy only shook his head. He was tall and robust, with curly, straw-colored hair.

'It's Master Bruno. Don't you remember him?'

'No.'

'When you were younger he often took you for an outing to the spring with Master Miguel and the señora, may she rest in peace. ...'

The boy shook my hand, and José insisted that I honor his home with my presence. 'Give us two glasses of vermouth, woman,' he said.

Hanging on the wall of the foyer were a sheepskin jacket, a canvas hat, and a shotgun.

'Yours?' I asked.

'Yes.'

'What gauge?'

'Twelve.' José held it by the stock and handed it to me.

'But one of these days I'm going to sell it. It kicks.'

The car arrived after one. I had gone up to the reservoir up the hill to see if I could find Miguel's hiding place, and I heard the tooting of the horn just as I was returning through the woods. A red Dauphine suddenly whirled into the terrace. From my vantage point I could hear voices and laughter. The car braked suddenly and stopped in the shadow of the eucalyptuses. A girl ran toward the gallery, and I recognized her from the wedding picture: it was Mara.

'Miguel! Where's Miguel?'

She was wearing blue jeans and a colored blouse, and her short hair and determined gestures gave her a charming, boyish appearance. When she saw me, she stopped but showed no surprise. 'Who are you?' she said.

A boy about twenty years old appeared behind her, leading a child by the hand. Mara pushed back a lock of hair from her forehead. I told her who I was, but she pretended not to hear me.

'And Miguel?' she asked.

'I haven't seen him,' I answered. 'I've looked for him at the reservoir and the stone bench but he's not there.'

'Then he must be writing in the cavern,' she said. She turned to the young man and introduced us. 'Come quickly,' she added. 'He's going to die laughing.'

Jorge and I followed her along the corridor and climbed the stairs of adobe to the attic. The attic ran the length of the top floor – it was our favorite refuge when we wanted to be alone to think – and its ceiling was all tiles and enormous wooden beams that sloped down the sides, following the shape of the roof. Mara pushed the first door to the left.

'Miguel,' she said. 'I bet you can't guess what's happened?'

Miguel was stretched out on the floor smoking in the midst of a pile of books, and he arched his eyebrows when he saw me. Mara told how the lifeguard had spent the whole morning eyeing her two-piece bathing suit and had finally come up to her and said, 'Miss, I've been watching you for a long time. If you come back again like this, I'll have to fine you.'

'I wish you could have seen his face,' she said. 'The poor fellow was all flushed, right, Jorge?'

Miguel got up from the mattress, laughing, and we embraced. He looked thinner and paler, as if prematurely old. His cheek touched mine, and I thought maybe it was his beard that made him look older.

'My husband always goes around looking like a slob,' said Mara, reading my thoughts. 'There's no way of getting him to shave. You've know him for a long time – maybe you can convince him. I've lectured him thousands of times, like those fat wives in the movies, but it didn't work. When he's caught up in some idea, no one can budge him.'

'Hygiene is a bourgeois virtue,' said Miguel. 'Perfume repels me.'

'You've always got a theory. We know, we know, you're smarter than everybody. We poor mortals understand nothing. But I'm warning you now: if you don't shave, you're sleeping with Jorge or your friend Bruno tonight. I'm fed up.'

Miguel took my arm, and we went down to the garden. In the gallery, a dark girl with Indian features was clearing bottles from the tables, and she said hello. Mara and Jorge had gone off to shower, and we sat down on a bench in the summer-house.

It was many years since we had been able to talk in peace, and I asked him about Armando and his book on the followers of Erasmus. I had been so impressed with his analysis of Renaissance culture that at the Sorbonne I had used it as a basis for my lectures. I told him I had reservations about the influence he attributed to Luis Vives, and Miguel stroked his beard and said his book was worthless. He had not really dealt with the most important problems, he said, and he tried to involve me in an argument to prove his point.

'For every nail one hits on the head there are a hundred others. . . . I still don't understand why people liked it.'

'What are you working on now?' I asked.

'Nothing,' Miguel answered. 'I'm studying.'

Mara came to tell us that the appetizers were served, and we made ourselves comfortable on a sofa in the gallery in front of a tray full of clams, stuffed olives, and canned asparagus. Jorge uncorked a bottle of Castell de Remey. Mara was wearing a linen skirt that went well with her tanned legs. The record player played *South Rampart Street Parade*, and Miguel talked about wines and said that those from Rioja lacked personality.

'Are you surprised?' exclaimed Mara. 'Wine and hunting are the only things that interest him.'

During dinner I talked about the lectures I had given in Oslo, Heidelberg, and Paris. I knew Miguel's sense of humor very well, and I dusted off several sure-fire stories. Miguel laughed but not once did I have the feeling that we had made contact. Our old intimacy had disappeared. Mara, on the other hand, listened with enjoyment, and when the dark girl came with the fruit, she suddenly turned to Jorge.

'Listen,' she said. 'Now that we're together, why don't you explain to Bruno how your thesis is getting along?'

Miguel looked at her somewhat surprised, and Jorge blushed. There was a moment of silence.

'I haven't progressed much, I'm afraid,' said Jorge.

'We know that already,' Mara broke in. 'But don't you have any ideas?'

'I've been thinking over what you said ...' Jorge said to Miguel.

'Where?' Mara insisted. 'On the beach?'

Jorge stammered in confusion, and Mara told me that his parents had let him come to Mas on condition that he work with Miguel. 'He's been here three weeks, and he'd rather go swimming with me instead of studying.'

Mara served us coffee in the gallery – the record this time was *Saint James Infirmary* – and after a few minutes conversation she announced that she was going out on the terrace to read.

'You come too,' she said to Jorge. 'Miguel and Bruno have a lot to talk about. Men should be alone to talk.'

Miguel lit a cigarette with the end of another and suggested a walk. The glare of the sun was hard on the eyes, and I went for sunglasses. When we came out, Mara was lying on a lounge chair reading. Jorge had taken refuge in the summer-house and was absorbed in the view.

For a few seconds we walked under the trees in the direction of the stone bench. The cork trees had recently been dehusked, and their bare knotty trunks curled into tormented gestures. As we got closer to the ravine the heat lessened. The top of the mountain sheltered us from the sun. Mistletoe covered the branches of the oaks and the vegetation thickened. On the slope Miguel and I had constructed a hunting blind with branches from madrone trees and boxthorn in order to ambush the partridges that lighted near the sluice. While we looked for its

remains, Miguel cocked an ear and stopped. The partridges cackled as they drank and, as if aware of our
presence, noisily took flight and hid in the chestnut trees.

'One of these days we can go hunting with José,'
said Miguel. 'Downstream there are lots of wild
pigeons.'

'What about the law?' I asked.

'The warden is half deaf and always stays in town. The
only problem is the Civil Guard.'

We had crossed the chestnut wood, and after following
the sandy river bed we came to the spring. Ferns and
brambles obstructed the path, and we had to advance
very slowly. Doves cooed in the bushes. Miguel drank a
few sips of water and we sat on the stone slab that served
as a table.

'You remember?' he murmured.

The spring brought back memories of childhood, and
I looked in vain for an inscription that I had engraved
in the trunk of a plane tree with my knife.

'How is Armando?' I asked. 'Can one see him?'

'Mara goes every week with Dora.'

'Dora?'

'His friend. A very intellectual girl. If you'd like to go
with them . . .'

Miguel was smoking absent-mindedly, and I didn't
insist.

'Life abroad does well by you,' he added, a little aggres-
sively. 'Is it true you're getting married?'

'Me? Who told you that?'

'I don't know. Someone who came down from Paris.
He said: "Bruno is living with a French woman and
they're getting married." '

'That's the first I've heard.'

'Aren't you living with a French woman?'

'Yes.'

'Well, he must have invented the part about the wedding.'

It seemed to me that he wanted to say something more: his eyes shone for an instant, as if he were going to confide in me, but he changed his mind and a shadow crossed his face.

On the way back to Mas – Miguel sank his hands in his pockets and told me all about his projects – we found Jorge seated on the edge of the pond. The frogs had dived under the green scum, and he was thrashing at the plants on the bottom with a cane stalk.

'Dora is coming tonight with Alvaro and Luis,' he announced. 'They just phoned a minute ago.'

I went to rest in the gallery and read an adventure novel in one sitting. Mara went out for a walk in mid-afternoon, after giving the baby a bottle. Jorge offered to accompany her, but she said she wanted to be alone. 'You men are such egoists,' she exclaimed. 'If you had a son and a house to take care of, you'd appreciate the value of silence.' Jorge bent his head sulkily, and I watched Mara as she disappeared into the woods.

Then Jorge threw himself on the sofa and complained that his studies were monotonous and boring. He had only been studying one year for his degree in Romance languages, he said, but he loathed every subject. The professors just weren't any good. As soon as they got tenure, they began to live like parasites and sent a substitute. He had been suspended by a measly assistant with no imagination: 'You have to be really gullible to listen to him. If it'd been somebody like Miguel, it would have been another story.'

Jorge talked on vehemently and confided that he planned a trip to France and Italy as soon as it was possible. 'Do you think I'll be able to earn a living in Paris?' he asked.

'That depends on what you call earning a living,' I answered.

'Oh I'd be happy with anything. . . . Just enough to eat and have a place to sleep. I have a friend who manages with a dishwashing job.'

I went out with him at dusk to stretch my legs. The sky had been getting darker and darker, and while we contemplated the gray hazy sea, it began to drizzle. The shadows in the valley came to life. A woman started calling loudly, and we could hear a cart creaking monotonously. Near us a dog began to bark. The girl who had served us at midday climbed up the hillside with a bundle of wood on her shoulder, and Jorge squinted to see her better.

'Who is she?' I asked. 'Does she live with the tenants downstairs?'

'She's one of the daughters,' he explained. 'Haven't you been to see them?'

We walked down to the vegetable garden, and as I looked over the wall, I could make out José's silhouette gathering fodder in the garden. The rain had only served to settle the dust, but clouds completely covered the sky. The girl passed in front of us and greeted us with a smile. Her legs were robust and well formed, and for a few seconds my eyes delighted in the suggestive path of her curves. A woman – the mother, no doubt – sat on the stoop plucking a chicken.

José came close to talk, and we went into the yard. The tenant's house was full of girls who had just returned from working in the fields like men, and I admired their lustiness and animal vigor. The youngest was sifting flour, and the third disappeared into the dim rooms inside and came back with her two hands full of rice.

'How many will there be tonight?'

'Seven,' Jorge answered.

'Put another fistful in,' said the mother.

The kitchen hadn't been changed at all. The dark girl – her sisters called her Lolita – piled the kindling wood on the backlog in the fireplace and started a fire. The flames gave her Indian features color, and she offered to prepare tea.

'No thanks,' said Jorge. 'We'll drink something upstairs.'

The two households were joined by an inside staircase. Jorge turned on the light in the kitchen and brought out two Coca-Colas from the cork-lined wine cooler.

'We could have a cuba libre,' he said. 'How about it?'

Miguel was talking to his wife in the garden. As I came up, Mara smiled and asked if I felt at home at Mas. 'It's terrible,' she murmured. 'Miguel and you have a whole past together, a thousand shared memories. Since you arrived, I feel out of it, excluded. . . .' Miguel listened to her in silence, and I saw that he had shaved. Jorge appeared with the gin and Coca-Colas. 'Do you want a drink too?' he asked. The frogs in the pond began to tune up, and in a moment a tunnel of light flashed on the row of cypresses on the road and the begonias in flower pots on the balustrade.

'It's them,' said Miguel in a lugubrious voice.

A white Seat 600 stopped just a few yards from us. Its headlights outlined the rough trunks of the eucalyptuses, and the people in the car got out, laughing excitedly. Mara introduced us and we all went into the gallery.

Armando's friend was a tall girl with ash blond hair, delicate lips, and huge eyes. She announced theatrically that she had gotten up on the wrong side of the bed and needed a few drinks to get in shape. 'We stopped in every town on the way to drink vodka,' she said.

'The three of us are half crocked,' Luis added.

'What do you want to drink?' asked Mara.

Luis said that alcohol made him lustful and asked about Lolita.

'Lolita has a fiancé,' Mara warned.

'Feudal lords slept with the daughters of their tenants. Why can't we go back to the Middle Ages?'

Alvaro told us a story of someone named Andrés who roamed his lands on horseback dressed as Robin Hood and brought his peons together every Sunday in the chapel and obliged them to listen to motets by Father Vitoria.

'You ought to do as he did,' Alvaro concluded.

Mara said that they had more important things to do.

'It's true, it's true,' exclaimed Luis. 'Do you know what's the most fashionable thing to do in Barcelona today?' Since we all remained quiet, he announced, 'Buy a jukebox like the ones in bars for your own home. My sister knows some characters who've got one.'

'Who supplies the coins?' asked Mara. 'Guests?'

'Their children,' said Luis. 'It seems they're very studious and their grandmother gives them twenty *duros* every week.'

'My sister always breaks open Arturo's piggy bank and takes the money,' said Dora. 'When they're broke the kids help them out.'

'That's the way it should be,' said Alvaro. 'Teach your kids about life. They shouldn't even trust their own mother.'

Their nonsense began to tire me, and I went to the kitchen with Mara. Lolita was hurrying back and forth with trays and plates. She said there was rice in the oven and chicken giblet fricassee. 'Do you need anything else, ma'am?' Mara said no and, when we were alone, asked what I thought of Dora. 'She's very good-looking, isn't she?'

I told her that she wasn't bad, and she looked at me out of the corner of her eye.

'That's curious,' she murmured. 'All the men say they don't like her. I find her very attractive. She has the beauty of an old medallion, perhaps a little cold. . . . I don't know. I may be wrong.'

While she uncorked the bottles of Perelada, she explained that Dora was a good girl but incapable of being alone for a second. Since she'd met Armando, she lived only for him.

'What does she do?' I asked.

'She's studying at the Theater Institute. I'm sure she'll get ahead. She's got real talent.'

Mara added that she appreciated her good qualities, but often was bothered by her. 'She'll talk to you the whole blessed day about Armando as if there were no other man in the world. Miguel can't stand her.'

When we returned to the gallery, Alvaro put on the Marlene Dietrich record. Jorge looked at me with a sullen expression. Dora had taken over the sofa, and made a childish face. 'No one has complimented me on my hairdo. I spent more than three hours in front of the mirror changing my make-up and nail polish. I wanted to look the way they did in the days when they did the charleston.'

'Bangs look well on you,' said Mara.

Miguel looked at the floor dully and then suddenly perked up. 'Anything that covers your face up is good for you,' he said.

Dora laughed without meaning to, and there was a moment of silence.

'Why don't we have supper?' Mara suggested.

Miguel had infected us with his melancholy, and the conversation at the table lagged. Mara repeated her story about the lifeguard, and Alvaro and Luis two of the latest jokes popular in Geneva (they both were studying there). Jorge couldn't hide his sullen feelings. The baked rice turned out tasteless and dry, and Miguel pointed to the tray and said it made him feel sad.

'It looks like a landscape in Castile,' he said.

Mara gave him an angry look, and when we finished coffee, I heard them arguing in the garden.

'They're always bickering,' Alvaro whispered. 'Then they go to bed together, and the next day they're good friends again.'

Dora said that Armando and she also quarrelled – with and without cause – but after each fight they loved each other more than ever. 'Poor darling Armando. . . . What can he be doing at this hour?'

'Sleeping,' answered Alvaro. 'What the hell do you expect him to be doing?'

It began to drizzle again, and Miguel and his wife came back in. If I remember rightly, Mara was smiling. Moths flew round the light bulb. There was a fresh breeze blowing, and Miguel said he was going to bed.

I too was dying to go, but the others insisted that I stay a while longer. 'We've come to Mas to dig in for good,' said Dora. 'We're staying until we get thrown out.'

The Perelada went down like water, and after the fourth glass, I discovered I was tight. Mara and Luis argued about what to do on Midsummer Night's Eve. Dora was still listening to Marlene Dietrich. Finally, I gave them the slip and slept like a log until dawn.

When I went out in the garden, there were dewdrops on the flowers. The gallery door was open, and I saw Mara sweeping the fallen leaves off the other end of the terrace. She was wearing a man's shirt and jeans and asked if I had been able to sleep.

'Very well,' I said.

'Didn't the uproar keep you up?'

'What uproar?'

'Alvaro and Luis sang smutty songs until four.'

'Well, I didn't hear them.'

'That's good. I was really worried about you. I thought, if they wake Bruno, he'll leave for France tomorrow without saying good-bye.'

While she swept, I explained that I always slept soundly.

'I got used to noise in Paris,' I said. 'And you? How many hours did you sleep?'

'I'm an incorrigible early riser,' she sighed. 'Poor Miguel has had to bear that cross too. I can't help it. At seven I *have* to be up.'

Mara gathered the leaves into a wicker basket and pointed to the cork trees. 'I love to work in the soil,' she said. 'Many people take me for an intellectual, but I'm really a complete primitive. I've cleared the whole hillside. The wood I pick up comes in handy in the house. That way I save a few pennies every month – that I squander on myself.'

The day called for a walk, and I took a short cut through the carob grove. At that hour the prickly pears were greener than ever. The rain had washed the leaves, and the pears were beginning to ripen. The manure was piled up in the same place as usual, on the right side of the path. I liked its sharp odor and stopped to admire the cane field and the ravine. Some steps beyond there was a seedbed where José planted cabbage before transplanting it to the vegetable garden. A goat tied to a rope was nibbling the acacias. I descended to the ravine, skirting the dry fields, in search of José. A red-headed young man was spading the soil on the edge of the orchard. When I passed, he said good day and told me that José had gone to town in the two-wheeled carriage to shop. He had a thick Andalusian accent and was astounded to see me up so early.

'When do you usually get up?' I asked.

'That depends on the season,' he answered. 'In summer at five, in winter a little later.'

'And yet you think I'm up early?'

'With us it's different, sir. We poor are used to it.'

At Mas the guests were stirring little by little. Lolita served breakfast on the terrace, and around ten Miguel, Jorge, and Luis showed up. Mara prepared buttered toast and kept an eye on the baby splashing in the plastic pool. Damiana came with a small basket of figs. 'They're very fresh, ma'am,' she said. 'If you'd like cherries, I'll bring some of them too.' Lolita's older sister spied on Damiana from the footbridge, and when the two left, Mara said that she was fed up with advice and gossip and complained that Miguel was no help. 'He just blithely scratches his belly and I have to take charge of every thing. . . .'

'What do you want me to do?' Miguel said. 'Don't you see it's useless?'

'You should decide that,' Mara answered. 'You're the man.'

Dora emerged in a nightgown looking like a ghost, and Mara explained that the tenants down below had had words with Damiana at the wash place and called her a liar and a thief. 'I tell you, if this goes on this way, it'll

end badly. The day you least expect it, they'll fight it out
with knives.'

While the others got ready for the beach, Miguel took
my arm and led me to the gallery. I preferred to sunbathe at the sunny spot above and went to my room
to get my bathing suit. When I returned, Dora and
Jorge were waiting on the footbridge. Luis was honk-
ing impatiently. Mara asked me if I was going with
them.

'No,' I said.

When I explained that I wanted to stay and swim in
the reservoir, Mara changed her mind and said she'd go
with me.

'Good, I'll stay too,' said Jorge.

'Bruno and I want to talk by ourselves,' Mara said
brusquely. 'If the beach bores you, go work with Miguel.'

The scene at the pond was unforgettably familiar to
me. The ground was covered with dead leaves, and the
air smelled vaguely of thyme. Many summers, Miguel,
Armando, and I had baked in the sun for hours and
hours until we were almost stupefied. The place was a
real oven; no breeze ever blew there.

Mara smeared my back with suntan lotion, and for a
long time I listened to the bees buzzing in the madrone
trees. Mara lay face down, her cheek on her robe. She had
undone the strap of her bikini, and I noticed that the
tan of her back was even.

'It's curious,' she murmured. 'From Miguel's stories I
could see you very distinctly. Every time you wrote him,
I read the letters and tried to imagine what you were like.
... I know that reading other people's mail isn't nice but
I can't help it. ... It's a terrible defect.'

The sun beat down on us, and I half closed my eyes in
order to look at her. Mara kept her eyes closed with an

expression of childish abandon. Between us there was a spike of lavender, and I took a flower and tasted it.

'How did you find Miguel?' she asked suddenly.

'I don't know,' I answered. 'It's difficult to explain. I think he's changed a lot.'

Mara arched her eyebrows. Her small, black eyes stared into mine. 'I don't know what to do with him any more. Every day he seems a little more removed from the world. He's built a refuge just for himself and doesn't leave it. . . . You should talk to him; you've known him since he was a boy. He would confide in you more easily. It's impossible for me.'

As she got up she tied the top of her suit around her breasts. The song of the cicadas seemed to spring from the earth itself. A horsefly landed on her knee and she chased it away with a shake of her leg.

'Has he said anything about Armando?'

'Just a few words.'

'He doesn't show it, but he suffers a lot. I think he loves Armando more than anyone else in this world. I try to help him shake it off, but, let me tell you, Miguel is difficult. If you don't go after him in his lair, he won't make a move.'

Mara stood up, naked to the waist, and dived in the pond. The water spiders on the surface skittered away. After splashing around for a few seconds, her head came up a dozen yards away, and she began to head away from me.

The glare blurred my vision, and I dived in too. The greenish water hardly allowed the light through. When I came back up, I tried to stay afloat by wiggling my hands. Above me the sky shimmered, blue and white. Everything made you want to close your eyes and just float till you were tired of it.

On the way back to the clearing where we sunbathed, Mara explained that Miguel needed distractions, to see people, and that my coming was exactly what she would have prescribed. Jorge's presence had been useful, too, she added, but Jorge was still a child, with all the faults and virtues of a nineteen-year-old who was also an only child.

'The poor fellow reacts like a real adolescent. For some days now he's got it into his head that he's in love with me, and there's no way of convincing him that he's fooling himself. His mother spoiled him by giving in to all his whims, and he gets furious because I don't take him seriously.'

Mara squirted on more suntan lotion from a little plastic bottle and said all men acted like kids: 'I don't understand why it's such trouble for you men to talk. Armando and Miguel are the best brothers in the world, but when they're alone they never have a serious discussion. We women are much more open than you.'

Miguel came up to bathe at one, and when the gang returned we got together on the terrace for an apéritif. Just like the afternoon before, there were clams, asparagus, olives, and two bottles of Castell de Remey. The eucalyptuses cast shadows on the table. Dora wore a sheath with a low waistline and said that there were twenty-two more hours to go until she could visit Armando. Jorge had received a telephone call from his parents telling him to meet them at Sitges and, as she passed behind him, Mara threw her arms around his neck and murmured affectionately in his ear.

'What are you going to do?' Luis asked.

'I don't know,' said Jorge. 'I feel like dropping everything and going to France.'

Mara supervised the rituals, and after lunch and coffee,

I went to my room for the siesta. When I woke up, it was past five. The sun from the window was reflected on the ceiling, and I listened drowsily to the buzzing of the flies.

In the gallery the record player was playing a lullaby of Atahualpa Yuanqui's. Dora looked at me with her sad, gazelle eyes. 'They're Armando's records,' she murmured. I sat down at her side, and she handed me a pile of records: Paul Robeson, French songs, *The Threepenny Opera*. She was wearing the same bangs as the night before, and I was surprised to see tears running down her cheeks.

'Gin makes me cry,' she said in a quavering voice.

Mara approached from the footbridge with Jorge, and when she saw Dora, she got angry.

'Will you stop masturbating once and for all!'

Dora powdered her face, but her hands shook and gave her away. Suddenly, unable to contain herself, she burst into sobs and fled down the hall. Mara went after her immediately.

'What's happened to her?' asked Jorge.

'I don't know. She was crying when I got here.'

Alvaro and Luis came over and asked what was happening, and Jorge explained that Dora's nerves were bad.

'She drinks coffee all day. Then, in order to sleep, she needs whole boxes of sleeping pills.'

Miguel was poring over his dictionaries in the Cavern, and I went up and told him bluntly what Mara had said about Jorge. The setting sun gilded the ceiling's low beams. Miguel lit a cigarette and gave a mocking smile.

'Jorge is a sentimentalist. His mother is in love with him and women fascinate him. . . . Mara and I like him a lot.'

As usual he put me off with his irony, and I didn't want to insist. On the terrace, the gang was getting ready to go to town to shop. Dora spoke in a shrill voice and laughed very loudly. 'Are you coming with us?' asked Mara. I said I didn't feel like it and went out to the stone bench in the summer-house.

In a while José came to open the floodgate of the pond; he was barefoot and his shirt tails were out. He told me that the pipes often got clogged, and I went with him to the vegetable garden to see if the water was flowing.

'Someone was asking about you this morning,' he said.

'Who?'

'Remember Luciano?'

'Yes.'

'When you wrote Miguel, I told him you were coming, and he said he'd like to say hello.'

'When are you seeing him again?'

'Tomorrow I'm going in the cart to get feed. If you want, we can go by his house.'

'Good. I'll tell Miguel and we three will go, like the old days.'

While we were walking to the garden, he talked about Luciano and his wife. According to him, the oldest daughter was a grown girl, and it was a pleasure to look at her. 'I tell you, it's worth the trip. The town boys are crazy about her.'

The water gurgled impetuously through the conduit, and José and the red-haired boy began to irrigate the garden. Years ago, Miguel, Armando, and I used to slosh around in the mud with them. I liked farm work, and it reminded me once again how stuffy and closed in Paris is. The water skirted the garden along the ridges to the other end of the plot and started down the asparagus frames. When it got to the end of the ditch, José shut the entrance with the hoe and opened the next one.

'In town they often think of you,' he said. 'I play pool

at Tano's bar every week, and not a Sunday goes by without someone mentioning you.'

In a slow, deliberate voice he brought me up to date after five years' absence: Marcos had married Telmo's sister; Jordi had three sons and was the same weak fellow as always; Martin had died in an accident in the quarry in the ravine, and his sister – the one who was crazy – had committed suicide by drinking a bottle of lye.

'And the Andalusian?' I asked. 'What's become of him?'

'Oh,' he said. 'He's still the same. The other day his wife found some nylon panties he had bought for his girl friend and gave him a drubbing that almost crippled him.'

Miguel seemed delighted with my suggestion, and we decided to organize a hunt the following day at Luciano's house. We were lying down in the garden listening to the croaking frogs from the pond, a little groggy with the heat.

'We can shoot pigeons, or go to the other end of the mountain and see if we find rabbits.'

'It's been six years since I've squeezed a trigger,' I said.

'It's like walking,' answered Miguel. 'You can't forget. Besides, Armando's shotgun is a good one.'

The moon was in its fifth night that night, and as if anticipating the summer heat, silent flashes of lightning intermittently lit up the mountain. Mara and the others came back around ten. As it took the turns, the car honked its horn furiously, and Lolita put on the lights in the gallery.

'No more peace and quiet,' said Miguel. 'Sometimes I wonder why they don't stay in Barcelona if they like excitement so much.'

The Dauphine parked next to the footbridge, and

when he got out, Alvaro announced that he was famished. 'You look worn out,' said Dora. 'What's the matter with you two?' Mara stroked Miguel's hair and kneeled on the ground between the two of us. 'Bruno is a quiet lady-killer,' she said. 'He got a letter today from some French girl, and it smells of good perfume. Here you are, my boy,' she added, handing me a blue envelope, 'and take pity on the poor native girls here because we're hopeless sentimentalists, and a city slicker like you would sweep us off our feet. . . .'

In my room, while changing for supper, I read Régine's letter. She said that her father was doing better ('*aucun espoir d'héritage*'), and sadly described the provincial life in Blaye and the undistinguished landscape in Garona. '*Réponds-moi vite, je t'en supplie,*' she wrote on the margin of the sheet, and I decided to do so before I went to bed.

Mara had opened two bottles of Perelada and called on Miguel to intervene to make Jorge obey his parents. Jorge remained silent and taciturn. 'My mother insists on thinking I haven't been weaned yet,' he murmured. 'I'm sick of being treated like a child.' Dora said he should be reasonable. 'Tomorrow I'll go with you to Stiges if you want. It's Armando's visiting day.' Mara approved of her idea, and after much talk, it was decided that Dora and Jorge would leave in the morning by car and meet at mid-afternoon in some café in Barcelona, if Jorge had managed to win over his parents.

'And you?' asked Mara, turning to me. 'Why don't you go with her?'

'Armando asked me not to bring anyone,' said Dora. 'The poor fellow wants to talk to me alone. But I'll tell him you're here. If you want to give him some message. . . .'

After supper I went walking with Mara in the garden. A cool light breeze had risen, and heat lightning would at intervals outline the sinuous crest of the mountain.

'What does your friend say? Is she dying without you?'

I laughed and told her who Régine was, but she interrupted me: 'I warn you, you'd better not answer me. I'm impossibly curious. Give me an inch and I'll take a mile, as they say. If you don't watch it, you're a goner.' Her eyes shone like a cat's.

'Have you talked openly with Miguel?' she said after a while.

I told her about the brief conversation we'd had that afternoon and said that the next day we were going to see Luciano.

'Miguel needs to get out,' said Mara. 'I'm sure just your presence helps him a lot. You don't know how happy I am you've come.'

'Me too, Mara.'

'Yes?' she said. 'And which one of us makes you happy? Him or me?'

'Both,' I answered. 'I'm at home with you both.'

'For pity's sake, don't lump us together. Miguel and I love each other very much, but we're two different persons. I've never been able to put up with the notion that I must be identified with him, as if I were an object. I want people to like me for myself.' Mara lit a cigarette and blew a smoke ring. 'Oh, I know that we wives should be little homebodies and not open our mouths unless someone asks our opinion, but what do you expect? I'm the way I am. I always said to Miguel: if you don't like it, I'll go, and peace be with you.'

Dora came to look for me, and we went to the gallery. Jorge had drunk half a bottle of gin and could hardly stand. When he saw us, he stared at me with bloodshot eyes.

'What's the matter with you?' asked Mara.

'Nothing,' Jorge muttered. 'I'm bored.'

'Nineteen-year-olds who get bored deserve a spanking.' Mara filled a glass with gin to the very top and offered it to him. 'Here, if you want more, drink. No one's stopping you here.'

Jorge took the glass. His wrist shook.

'It'll harm him,' Dora protested.

'Let him do what he wants. He's old enough to know that.'

'I'm no kid. . . .'

'Give me your hand then. I'll fix an Alka-Seltzer for you and tomorrow you'll be like new.'

They went down the hall, and Miguel said that Jorge was undisciplined. 'Every difficulty looks like a mountain to him,' he explained. 'Every time he's about to go see his family he gets drunk and talks of suicide. The word tomorrow has no meaning to him. He lives only for today.' Dora said that Armando reacted just the same way. 'Do you remember when he had to do his military service?' No one answered, and I took advantage of the silence to say good night and went to my room to write.

Early next morning, Damiana knocked on the door and said that José was waiting to leave. 'Master Miguel is having breakfast on the terrace,' she added. I'd slept soundly all night, and I showered and shaved as quickly as I could.

Outside, the sun shone from time to time, and winds swept the shredded clouds. Miguel was drinking coffee, absorbed in a newspaper. Dora and Jorge were also getting ready to leave. Dora had painted herself up like a mask, with light rose lips and enormous rings of eye shadow. 'I'll ask Armando if you can come next time,' she promised. Jorge paced up and down, and when he got into the car, Mara said something consoling.

'Let's go,' said Miguel brusquely. 'Hurry up.'

I drank my coffee in one gulp, and while the Seat made the turn we walked toward the corral. The freshness of the morning was pleasant; once in a while the air smelled of wet grass. José had harnessed the mule, and we helped him tie it up to the cart.

'Hey,' he said. 'Are you sleepy?'

He was wearing a white shirt and navy blue pants, and there were traces of soap on his freshly shaved cheeks.

'A little bit,' I answered. 'You get perverted immediately around here.'

José ran to get the sacks of feed, and I whiled away the time examining the mule's harness. The cart was the same one Doña Luz used on Sundays to go to church. The top was a little faded, but I noticed that the seat upholstery was still intact. The mule pawed impatiently, and Miguel said she was rebellious and full of mischief.

'Her former owner did not train her well.'

'Around here we've got a saying: a man who can't break in his horses, can't rein in his woman either,' said José.

'Who sold it to you?'

'Can't you guess? . . . Jordi.'

'Does he have horns?'

'*Hombre!*' laughed José, showing his teeth. 'More than a bushel of snails.'

We got into the cart, and as soon as the mule began to trot happily, José explained that Martina had eyes for every man, and their youngest son had been sired by an

Andalusian who was staying at her house. 'He's a collier who works on the other side of the mountain. He's been living with them for a year.'

'And Jordi? What does he say?'

'Nothing. The young men in town needle him, but he always has some good reason to fool himself, and he puts up with it. The poor man is used to it by now. If I were to tell you what he's had to put up with since he got married, we'd have stories until nightfall.'

The path snaked among the carob trees. The prickly pears formed a thick hedge at the foot of the slope, and near the stream it was cooler. I saw a bed of melons in one of the gardens. The mule often broke into a gallop, and José continually had to pull on the bridle. When we arrived at the watercourse, he turned the wheel to the limit. The water ran into the ruts in the path, and when the brakes gripped the wheels they made a rough, unpleasant sound.

'A good year,' I said, pointing to the stream.

'Yes. Luciano has built a new reservoir to dam up the water. And yet last winter not a drop fell. The village priest had to bring the saint around at least twice. . . .'

At the crossing, we gave the right of way to a cart with yellow side poles. The mule driver wore a coarse apron, and José and he exchanged some words in Catalan. From there on the path was in good condition. The cane hid the view completely, and once in a while the mule would stretch his neck and swipe one, paying no attention to José's curses and lashes.

Luciano's house was a good half mile down the bed of the ravine. To reach it we had to cross the cane field, and it suddenly came into view, looking mossy and damp, in the middle of a grove of walnut trees. The owners had built the house at the start of the century to use as a poultry farm, but after spending a fortune in useless but expensive improvements, they finally rented it after the war. Luciano had come up from the south looking for work and had settled there with his family. While we skirted the little walnut grove, José explained that thanks to Luciano the owners had been saved from ruin.

Our arrival woke the house from its sleep. The dogs welcomed us with loud barking, and María stuck her head out the door and called her husband. A boy ran out of the straw rick. Luciano was working in the fenced-in yard with the hired boys, and when he saw us, he came and kissed Miguel on both cheeks.

Luciano was short, with strong arms and heavy, almost Moorish features. He wore a squarish mustache, long sideburns, and a dark beret slightly cocked to the right. His eyes always had an ironic gleam. He kissed me too, smiling, and María dried her hands on her apron and we embraced.

'Come, go on in,' he said. 'We have to celebrate this reunion.'

Near the door there was a tiny garden with amaranths and sunflowers; the dogs sniffed us and wagged their tails. Luciano's daughter had run off behind the pigsty and María explained that she was ashamed to have us see her dressed in everyday clothes.

'She's very flirtatious,' she said. 'She's got all the boys in town hanging around.'

The foyer served as a dining room, and we sat down around the table. Hanging from the beams of the drying room were strings of onions and bunches of grapes. Luciano uncorked a bottle of Tio Pepe and filled the glasses. Neither his wife nor he had changed during my absence. María looked as young as ever. He was the same good man he'd always been.

'How is France?' he asked.

I told him how things were going, while he scrutinized me with his restless eyes and nodded approvingly several times. Then we talked about Armando and the young people, and María sat with us, along with her two youngest children, and said that she had never seen anything like it.

'It just doesn't seem possible. I still don't know how we're able to get on.'

Luciano said that you couldn't swim and keep your clothes on at the same time. 'If you really must know, I guess it's our fault. . . .'

'Of course it is,' María said vehemently. 'Do you remember Font's friend? Manuel gave us all sorts of excuses, and now you see. It's already been a year.'

It was the kind of conversation that always went on at Tano's bar, and Miguel too seemed younger and kept looking at Luciano with shining eyes.

'How long are you staying?' asked María.

'Two weeks.'

'Next Sunday we're going hunting,' said Miguel. 'Come for us at six with the dogs.'

'Remember the last time we went together?' said Luciano.

'Yes.'

'It was the mushroom season at the end of October or the beginning of November. Armando filled a knapsack by himself, and then we got drunk among the pines.'

'We were happy then.'

'Yes,' murmured Miguel in a muted voice. 'We were happy.'

At lunch time, Mara said that she had spent the most delightful morning of her life. 'As soon as you left, I went up to the pond and sunbathed nude for four hours. I don't know if you've ever tried it. From now on, I think I'll always do it.' Since Miguel remained silent, she added that the company of men bored her. 'On the beach you're always bumping into some imbecile who stares or insists on starting a conversation. It's an absurd intrusion.'

Alvaro and Luis had gone to ambush Lolita while she watered the garden. Now they were taking it easy, sitting in easy chairs in the gallery, talking with enthusiasm about her robust curves and her profound contact with the soil and things.

'Lolita and her sisters have captured the truth of life,' said Alvaro. 'Their work permits them full self-realization.'

'We're contingent,' said Luis. 'But every gesture of theirs, on the other hand, reveals the essence of the world. They're absolutely necessary.'

'They'd gladly change places with us, contingent or not,' said Miguel.

'Yes,' Mara broke in. 'Why don't you develop calluses like they have?'

'Because it would be an intellectual decision and consequently false. One cannot understand and also *be* at the same time.'

'We intellectuals operate in a vacuum,' said Luis. 'They really exist and don't know it.'

'Explain that to the workers,' said Miguel. 'You earn fifty pesetas a day but you're essential, and although we look rich, we're contingent. You'll see what they'll answer.'

Alvaro said workers weren't rooted in the soil either, and the discussion degenerated into a controversy about the relative merits of the country and the city. Finally, we were all fed up, and Mara suggested to me that we take a walk.

'We've got to take good advantage of the sun. Damiana said the sky is going to get cloudy again.'

We climbed up the highway shortcut in the shadow of the cork trees, and suddenly Mara stopped and lowered her head.

'I have to confess something terrible to you,' she said. Her face looked repentant but under her handsome, thick eyelashes her eyes shone with malice. 'Oh, I don't know where to begin. . . .' her look implored my help. 'Promise you won't hate me if I tell you.'

'I promise.'

'Good, I'll take your word. . . . This morning while you were out, I went into your room to pick up your soiled clothes and stole Régine's letter.' Mara dug into her jeans' pockets and handed it to me. 'There, there it is.'

I took it without thinking. She looked fixedly at the ground.

'I've acted very badly, haven't I ?'

'No.'

'Yes, I've acted very badly, and I know that you're going to think very badly of me. But I warned you yesterday – when I see a letter addressed to someone else I can't help myself.'

I assured her that curiosity was a normal thing and said I wasn't making any judgments.

'If you're saying that to be polite, it'll be worse for you,' she sighed. 'I want my friends to accept me as I am, with all my defects. Miguel always says that I oblige everyone to be sincere with me, and it's true. That's why he fell in love with me.'

On the other side of the highway, the cork trees covered the crest of the mountain, and we made a path through the gorse. Broom dotted the slope with yellow spots. The grapevines began immediately after, and when we arrived, an old man was turning over the ground in the furrows. It was Francisco, the keeper of the vineyard, with his shrewd face and his forelocks over his temples. When he recognized us, he took off his cap, and we talked of the days when Miguel, Armando, and I would steal bunches of muscatel, and he would run after us through the woods throwing stones.

On the left there was an enormous reservoir of water, and Mara sat down on the edge of it. The vista we commanded was well worth the ten minutes' walk. The highway snaked like a river of stones, and farther off, among the almond trees, Antonio and some child were knocking down almonds with a pole. The hills merged smoothly, their profiles against the sea. Behind us, the wind shook the vines, and I tore off a bunch of green grapes and tasted its sourness.

'You haven't told me what you think of the letter,' I said, breaking the silence.

Mara was chewing a fennel stalk, and she looked at her hands for a long time before answering.

'I don't know,' she murmured. 'It seems to me that your friend enjoys writing well. I got the impression that she had rewritten the letter several times, like a composition.'

I protested that in France all university students wrote that well.

'It's possible,' she admitted. 'What kind of woman is she? Emotional? Intellectual? Come on, tell me. ... You know that anything that concerns you interests me.'

Mara looked at me intently, as if she were expecting something infinitely precious from me.

'No, don't answer me,' she said suddenly. 'I am forcing you, and you should resist me. I ask only one thing. Show me her picture. It's awful to talk about someone without even knowing what she looks like.'

I showed her a picture of the two of us in Les Graus du Roi, and told her that she was much better looking in person.

'She's very pretty,' said Mara, after a few seconds. 'Of course a ladykiller like you must have a harem. Right? Oh yes, don't deny it. You men are impossible flirts.'

Dora and Jorge returned just before supper. I was in my room, reading the letter from Régine that José had brought from town, when I heard whispers and steps in the corridor. It was Jorge and Mara, and she put a finger to her lips and signalled me to come. Jorge said that Dora was a wreck after the visit, and he had made her drink a few cuba libres to get her in a good humor. Now she was a little drunk but much calmer.

'Why?' I said. 'What happened?'

'It seems Armando was in a bad mood, and you know how easily she falls apart. When I arrived, she was crying desperately and talking of suicide. Then we talked and I managed to convince her that it was all a strategy of Armando's to draw attention to himself. I told her that Armando is very jealous and is suffering because of this separation, and now she's almost feeling good. If she asks you anything, be careful. Try to help calm her down.'

Dora was stretched out on the sofa in the gallery, powdering her face, and discussing with Alvaro the possibility of adapting a play of Brecht's. Before her visit to Armando, she had gone to see an exhibition of Aztec masks, and she was thinking of showing them to the stage designer. 'They're completely primitive, you know. All simple lines and sober colors. They'd go well with the costumes, don't you think?' Alvaro said that the interpretation should be austere. Luis replied that the designer's plans were not austere, and there was a brief discussion about what elements would have to be sacrificed. In one corner Miguel smoked and looked at the ceiling.

Later, during coffee, Dora went out to the terrace and told me about her visit, just as Jorge had interpreted it for her. 'Armando's a bastard, and he put on a long face to make me suffer. I was perfectly aware of his trick, but I'm such an idiot that by the time I left I'd ruined half a dozen handkerchiefs.'

She went on at length and said that she had found him worse than the last time she saw him. 'But when I was leaving I said, see you soon, and he said, adios. What do you think that means?'

'I don't know,' I answered. 'Probably nothing.'

'He said adios as if he weren't ever going to see me again. . . . I've been thinking about it, and I've decided he just wanted to upset me. Don't you think so?'

'Who knows, he may have said it without thinking.'

'No, no,' she insisted. 'You don't know him well. I'm sure he said it on purpose.'

The sad voice of Bessie Smith was singing *Any Woman's Blues* in the gallery, and before going to bed, I listened to her alone, leaning on the railing of the footbridge with my eyes fixed on the stars of my childhood; the sky had cleared up, and they shone again through the eucalyptuses. When we said good night – every one was sleepy that evening – I gave Mara Régine's letter.

'Thanks,' she said with a smile. 'I see you've gotten to know me.'

Next morning, taking advantage of a trip of Alvaro's, I decided to spend the day in Barcelona. Miguel wanted me to go with him to town, but Mara intervened and said, 'Bruno must have some girl friend there. Don't you see that you're interfering with his plans?'

It was the exact truth, and as soon as we left behind the gray towns of the coast, I said that women possessed a curious faculty for divining things.

'No, they're not fortune tellers,' Alvaro answered. 'It's just that they're thinking about us continually and always surprise us.'

My friend's name was Gloria, and we had lived together a few months in a hotel in Montparnasse before I had met Régine. Gloria had gone to Paris on a scholarship to the *Institut Français,* and since she had returned to Barcelona I had hardly heard from her. Someone told me that she had broken up an old engagement and was making a living writing articles for a fashion magazine.

When I phoned her, she showed her joy by squealing like a girl and suggested that we go swimming at Barceloneta. At the appointed time, she appeared on the terrace of the Cosmos in striped slacks and a very showy blouse. Gloria wasn't exactly good-looking, but she was striking. She had dyed her hair blond, and hid her eyes behind sunglasses of a complicated kind in which I could see myself reflected as in a mirror.

'At last, a breath of air from Paris!' she said. 'If you only knew how bored I am!'

Lying on a bright colored towel (Gloria had brought a beach bag full of lotions and French magazines and even a tiny transistor), she explained that she was living a mediocre, provincial existence, and she had a long list of complaints about Barcelona and her work. 'You never run into anyone interesting, I swear. As soon as I can I'm going to Paris – even if it's as a babysitter.'

I was already sorry I had called her, and when we sat down across from each other at an eating stand, Gloria took my hand and said, 'Please, let's talk in French.'

I was obliged to obey, and when the waiter came over

to take our order, I noticed that she put on an accent and I realized she was trying to pass herself off as a foreigner. '*C'est drôle,*' she said. '*Je crois rêver.*'

When I got back to Mas – Gloria finally invited me to her studio and I slept with her until sundown – Mara and Jorge were out on the terrace, and she took my arm and led me to the eucalyptuses.

'Come on, tell me,' she said. 'How was your outing? Did you get what you wanted?'

I gave her a resumé of my day with Gloria, and she laughed excitedly. When Miguel came to announce that he'd poured apéritifs in the gallery, Mara clapped happily.

'Bruno is a Don Juan. I saw through him the first day. There's not a one that gets away. Go on, tell Miguel what you've told me. It's a great story.'

'Stories about fornicating don't interest me,' said Miguel, somewhat dryly.

'I've known that for a long time,' she answered. 'You don't have to announce it.'

Their fight went no further, but I saw that Mara was furious, and during supper neither of them said a word.

Up at the pond next day, while the others were in swimming, Mara broke the silence for the first time.

'Last night when everyone was asleep I wrote you an endless letter,' she said. 'Then I thought better of it and burned it.'

'A letter? Why?'

'I don't know. I felt depressed, lonely. I had the feeling that I was of no help to anyone, that I was exhausting myself doing useless things. I wanted to offer you my friendship.'

'We're friends already, Mara.'

'No, you don't understand me. I wanted to ask you if

you'd count on me. I know you men don't take such things seriously, but I don't care. You can't imagine what it is to struggle alone always. My friends believe I'm very strong because Miguel forces me to be, but every once in a while I swear I won't put up with this role. I'm tired of living with people weaker than I am. There are days when I'd give anything to get help, to have a man I could lean on. . . .'

Mara was talking with her eyes fixed on the ground, and she let a fistful of sand run through her hands. In the madrone tree, the bees buzzed monotonously.

'Miguel is in love with me and doesn't need anybody else. It's enough for him to live alone with me, and he doesn't understand that although I love him, I sometimes get tired of propping him up. I need some mature person to take care of me, and assume responsibility for me the way I do for him. He takes what I do completely for granted.'

Mara stopped as if she were expecting some interruption from me. In the pond Jorge thrashed his legs, making foam; splashes of water fell on us.

'Actually, what I've told you is of no importance. Forget it. All of us have to jump over the rough spots, and we eventually land on our feet like cats.'

Miguel came down the path wrapped in a blue robe, and we stopped talking. I had thought the two of us would take a walk after lunch, but Mara said that she was going to take a nap with Miguel, and they shut themselves up in their room. When they came out two hours later, Mara's cheeks were still burning, and she seemed in a fine humor.

We were in the gallery listening to Marlene's songs, and Miguel lay down on the sofa and said that the siesta and wine were the most progressive inventions in this world. Mara had sat down next to him, and she ran her hands through his hair.

'Pigs !' exclaimed Luis. 'Will you please act decently.'

Dora smiled and said that Armando and she always caressed each other that way too. Her comment exasperated Miguel. 'For God's sake !' he yelled. 'Don't you ever have an abstract idea ?'

Clouds darkened the sky, and I went to my room to write Régine. When I finished, there was no one in the gallery. Lolita was washing dishes in the kitchen, and I asked her for a Coca-Cola, just to see her lean down over the cooler and admire her generous thighs.

'It's going to rain,' she said, pointing toward the window. 'Every time the wind blows from the north it rains.'

At the moment the clouds were gathered behind the mountain, but the swallows were flying low and the strange quiet in the air presaged a coming storm. I found Luis throwing pebbles in the pond, and he told me that Mara and the others had gone to town to buy groceries. The pebbles would skip several times over the surface of the water before they sank and disappeared. Finally, Luis seemed to tire of his game and put his hands in his pockets.

'I'm in a mess,' he said.

I asked him why, and he told me. 'Because of Lolita. I think I'm in love with her, and I don't know how to tell her. Yesterday I spied on her and saw her kiss her sweetheart, and I didn't sleep a wink all night. Have you ever been jealous ?' I said yes, and he looked at me gratefully. 'The life I'm leading is for the birds. In Geneva I slept with a different girl every day, but I've never been really in love. Lolita is a moral, healthy girl. I swear I'd marry her right now.'

We went for a walk in the woods, and as we walked he asked my advice on how to propose.

'When I see her I don't know what to say. I feel like a twelve-year-old.'

I told him that was really what he was, but he wouldn't listen.

'Do you think she's in love with her sweetheart?' he asked.

'She goes out with him, so she must be interested.'

'I can't believe it. Have you ever seen him? I don't deny he's strong – he'd make two of me – but you should take a look at his face. His forehead is half an inch wide. She can't possibly love him. I'm sure it's a family arrangement.'

The Dauphine returned in the late afternoon. Luis and I were still in the garden talking, and Dora pointed to the low-flying birds.

'Have you noticed?'

'I think we'd better take the chairs into the gallery,' Mara suggested.

The wind shook the branches of the eucalyptuses, and just after we went inside there was a streak of lightning, followed by a violent clap of thunder, and the first drops began to fall. The squall came down the mountain like an immense curtain of water. The birds flew crazily, and suddenly Mara ran out into the garden while the rain beat against the windows and lightning lit up the sky. In a few minutes she returned, soaked to the skin. 'It makes you want to roar like Tarzan,' she said. 'Who wants to come out and get wet with me?' No one answered, and after telling us we were bourgeois and sissies, she finally went up to her room to change.

Later the rain turned into hail. The storm had formed puddles in the terrace and water gurgled down the slope like a river. The hailstones hammered at the French windows like a salvo of birdshot. At nine the electricity was cut off, and we ate by candlelight. Miguel and Mara snapped at each other about a badly uncorked bottle. The Castell de Remey was drunk so matter-of-factly that it might as well have been water, and we all got slightly drunk and recited poetry and sang in the dark gallery.

The thunder lasted late into the night. Huddled in my sheets, I listened to the noise of the wind, and two or three times a sudden noise – like the crack of a dry stalk of cane when it breaks – warned me a few seconds before the thick walls trembled that lightning had hit the lightning rod. Miguel and I would climb up to the attic when we were boys, but this time I couldn't help feeling scared. It was raining buckets outside, and Mas seemed a flimsy protection against the storm's violence. A little after three I heard a window blow open. Then, some one got up to close it – a candle fleetingly lit up the corridor – and finally I fell asleep.

After a storm the sky is bluer than ever and the air looks cleaner and clearer. When I got up, the sun was shining on the terrace and birds were chirping, recovered now from the fright of the night before. The earth had a strong smell. As I walked around the house I ran into José. He was carrying a spade on his shoulder, and I went with him to the ravine.

'Hail is worse than the plague,' he said. 'Three beds of lettuce that I planted – ruined!'

The water had opened cracks in the strawberry patch, and earth from the ditches was piled up on the edge of the river. José showed me debris piled up against the slope. The fruit orchards below were also flooded; he pulled his pants up to his knees and began to drain off the water with the spade.

'What a life!' he exclaimed. 'You can't let up a second. You look aside a moment and you're gored.'

Dora was having breakfast in the garden with the boys. Mara had gone for the mail, and I found another letter from Régine. There was also a color postcard with a view of Barcelona seen from Tibidabo.

Dear Bruno, the postcard said, *Rescue me from this desert of tedium. I want to meet new people, see interesting places. Je suis plus découragée que jamais. Gloria.*

Dora had dreamt that she and Armando were living in a flooded apartment and wanted our personal interpretation of her dream. I told her it was the logical result of the night's storm, but I didn't convince her. 'No, no,' she answered. 'This wasn't the first time I've dreamed that. I'm sure it means something.' Alvaro started a lecture on Freud and psychoanalysis, and when Lolita came to remove the tray, I saw that Luis blushed and looked away.

While I was shaving, I heard Miguel and Mara quarrelling in their room. I was getting used to their spats and closed the door. Miguel's objections to Mara's accusations got briefer, and then he left abruptly. Jorge was washing his hands in the bathroom, and he told me that Miguel had received a good offer from an American university. 'They're offering him a contract for six months for a short course on Erasmus,' he said. 'Mara wants him to accept.'

At mid-morning all of us except Miguel went up to the pond to swim. The water was covered with acorns and pine needles blown down by the wind. Mara lay at my side among the lavender and asked me when I was going to Barcelona.

'Barcelona?' I said. 'Why?'

'You men have hearts of stone. Didn't you read your

friend's postcard? The poor girl is pining away. I'd like to know what drug you give women to make them so crazy about you.'

I told her Gloria was just bored and ran after everyone, hoping to catch some unwary man.

'You're terrible,' said Mara. 'As soon as you get what you want from a woman, you throw her aside like a rag. What does it cost you to go see her for a few hours? Anyway, considering what you do with her, it shouldn't take such a great effort.'

Mara pretended to be angry and got up holding her bathing suit top with her hands.

'You've got to help me, Bruno,' she said. 'I don't want the others to see me in this mood. I joke and laugh about myself, but I know that you understand. . . . I swear I can't go on.'

She showed me the letter from the university in Berkeley and said Miguel refused to answer it.

'Why?' I asked. 'Would it take so much of his time?'

'No, it's not that. He's gotten used to my sheltering him from all difficulties, and the idea of leaving his lair frightens him. He's turned down more than four offers this last year to teach abroad. The Americans because they're Americans. The Catholics because they're Catholics. The Protestants because they're Protestants. He's always got some excuse to lie to himself and other people. The truth is he's afraid.'

'What can I do, Mara?'

'I don't know. You're a man and he'll listen to you. Tell him he can't live this way, avoiding his responsibilities. He has to make an effort for the sake of others; he's got to compromise a little with life. . . . When I met him he was interested in things, he liked to talk. Now he doesn't move from his cavern. He eats, sleeps, reads his

Latin dictionaries. . . . The less he likes people the more passionate he becomes about words.'

The sun gilded her tanned body, and I dived into the pond with her. The water had become cooler since the evening before. I swam rapidly toward the other shore and returned to the clearing. Then I rubbed my body with a towel and went up to the attic to see Miguel.

'I want to talk to you,' I said.

He was lying down on a straw bed smoking, and he arched his eyebrows ironically. 'I'm at your disposition, Father.'

He was joking, but I didn't laugh. I missed our old conversations, the intimacy we had once had.

'I don't want to meddle in your affairs, but your silence forces me to. Aren't you aware of it? Since I came we haven't been sincere with each other a single moment. We're like two strangers.'

'I see you've talked to Mara,' he said. 'Did she cry much?'

'It doesn't matter whether she cried or not. When I wrote you asking if I could come, I did it because I wanted to be with you. I've been here four days now and I don't know what the hell I'm doing here. If for some reason it doesn't please you, tell me and I'll get right out. But don't treat me like one of your guests.'

Miguel crushed his cigarette on the floor and turned away, so that his profile was to me. His voice was changed and he sounded hoarse. 'I've lost the capacity for joy, Bruno. I suddenly discovered that one day, and there's nothing to do about it. I don't know how I'm strong enough to go on. . . .'

Miguel fixed his sight on the window, and his face hardened again. There was a brief pause.

'Mara is intent on my giving those lectures in the

United States, but it's absurd. To start something like that you have to believe in it.'

'What are you going to do then?'

'Nothing.' His eyes shone in an indefinable way, and I knew he was going to put me off again. 'Do you remember Dale Carnegie's books?' He grimaced. 'I've found a motto too: Forge Your Own Dark Hopeless Future – what do you think of it?'

'Sinister,' I said.

'I'm delighted with it. I'm going to have it inscribed on my door for guests to read. That way they'll leave me alone.'

That's as far as I got. For the rest of the week Miguel hardly left his study, and the tension slackened. Jorge worked on his thesis in a corner of the gallery, and in the afternoon he went out with Mara for walks. Dora each day counted the hours before her next visit to Armando. Luis' love problems took up all our talk. Alvaro made frequent trips to his family in the Seat, and one night I went to Barcelona to sleep with Gloria. When we returned, Mara was sunbathing by the pond. Dora and Jorge were talking about Lolita, and Mara clapped her hands with joy and asked how everything had gone.

'Was it O.K.? Go on, tell me,' she said.

I said there was nothing to tell, but she looked at me with a disgusted grimace and asked if I had gotten what I wanted.

'Naturally,' I said.

'Men are the vainest creatures. To hear you talk you'd think that women queue up to go around with you. Things aren't that bad, my boy.'

Mara smiled teasingly, and while we drank Perelada in the garden, she told Miguel that my female clientele not only kept growing but seemed most satisfied with my service.

'I'm beginning to be tempted,' she added.

It was a sunny day, and after lunch I went to my room to rest. When I woke up, it was six. The heat and the sensuality of the siesta had left me dazed, and I went up to the pond to bathe. Mara was in swimming and waved to me.

'It's divine,' she called. 'I've never enjoyed it so much.'

I dived off the board, and when I came up, I saw Mara climbing the ladder and putting on the bottom of her suit. After a few minutes – the lukewarm water made one relax and loll – I joined her in the clearing. She was lying face up, and she crossed her arms over her breasts.

'Please,' she said. 'Promise you'll keep your eyes closed.'

I obeyed her and lay down among the rock-rose. The sun licked my eyelids softly and I listened drowsily to the bees in the madrone trees.

'Jorge is back to his old story,' she sighed. 'Yesterday he made me a regular proposition, just like the ones you see in the movies. Poor fellow. I don't know what to do to disillusion him. Do you think I should act tougher?'

'I don't know,' I said.

'You're a mature man and know what's what. Not him. He's just a little boy really, and he lives in a state of perpetual excitement. Imagine, when he was only fifteen, his mother already gave him money to go with women – on condition that he tell her everything. She's in love with him, obviously, and she's completely confused him with that kind of treatment.'

I said Jorge needed to try out his wings, but she cut me off.

'He doesn't know,' she said. 'Every time we leave him alone he does one silly thing after another. Last month the electricity went off the night before his exam, and he spilled a bottle of ink on the floor and cut his hand with a pen. He never knows what he's going to do the next minute. Every obstacle seems insuperable to him.'

I got up for my robe and was surprised to find Miguel. Mara instinctively covered herself with a towel. Miguel looked at us with a vague smile, and in the heavy silence that followed his appearance I had the ridiculous sensation that I was the husband.

'Am I disturbing you?'

'No,' murmured Mara. 'Actually I was just coming to tell you to come swimming. . . .' She seemed furious with herself because of the gesture she had made, and with a visible effort she took off her suit and dived in the water.

The next few days Miguel made no comment about the incident, but I noticed that he often talked ironically about my good looks and my abilities as a ladies' man.

We went out hunting Sunday just as we had planned. Luciano and José came to get us at dawn, and we followed the jumping, whining dogs to the chestnut grove. It was as if the calendar had been turned back. Luciano led the way, his shotgun under his arm, and even Miguel seemed happy. Before we got close to the conduit, partridges flew across the ravine. The sun rose between the oak trees, and José recalled the days when Armando invited the boys from town, and we would get together at the spring to roast chestnuts.

'It's your fault, Bruno,' he said. 'Since you left we've all scattered.'

'And Miguel?' I said. 'Why doesn't he invite you?'

'Don't you know the Catalan saying, *Home casat, burro espatllat*?' said José. 'A married man is like a spoiled donkey. Everybody around here knows it.'

The dogs began chasing hares, and we could hear them panting along the hillside. Miguel walked by my side, and once he suddenly raised his shotgun and shot twice at a wild pigeon. The concussion left me momentarily deaf, but I admired his aim and his sure reflexes. The bird flapped his wings, badly wounded. Luciano shot too but missed. The pigeon started to lose height and finally fell among the brambles, and the dogs wriggled through the underbrush to find it.

'Let's continue uphill,' said José. 'I'm sure there are others.'

Miguel stayed behind to get the game, and we headed off via the waterway. The dogs ran with their tongues hanging out, following mysterious scents. The vegetation in the ravine cut off much of our vision, and we climbed in spurts along plowed land toward the pines. There the landscape changed a little. The wild vines were getting green on the slope, and saplings covered the stumps in the olive grove. When the dogs found a rabbit, we fanned out. José and Miguel climbed uphill at a run, and I heard several shots. It was years since I had felt so happy. The medlars were beginning to ripen, and the yellow wheat showed harvest time was near. Frogs croaked in some pond. I felt like yelling to Miguel that his desperation was stupid, and I wanted us to throw ourselves down in the tall grass to look at the cloudless sky and at the birds flying back and forth.

Miguel and José returned with two rabbits, and in order to cover the whole mountain we decided to separate. Luciano and Miguel took a shortcut on the left, while José and I took the lane for carts that led to the farmhouses on the other side of the mountain; we were to meet at the top. José was carrying the three catches in his game bag and said that we ought to proceed carefully because of the Civil Guards. As we climbed, we could see the view of the coastline better. Woods, vineyards, hills undulated smoothly, with the blue sea as background. A tiny mule pack followed the capricious line of the highway, and below the pine trees, the chimney at Mas smoked. The silence was so profound that you could hear the faraway chug of a locomotive.

During my absence the wood had burned several times, and we went toward its center, bypassing the burnt areas. Chestnuts, oaks, and pines mingled their greens, hugging the side of the mountain. We crossed mushroom grounds, and I was sorry that it wasn't the season for them. Past the first farmhouse, moss girded the trunks of oak trees, and we listened to the echo of axes. On the side of the path there were stacks of firewood. José led us into thick vegetation, and in a few minutes we stopped in a clearing planted with corn. José showed me a place where a wild boar had been rooting, and we continued across the field, walking carefully among the rows of corn.

The landscape inland was very different. Monotonously green forests succeeded one another until you could see no more. Only the women introduced a note of color.

The colliers had burned brushwood in a clearing, and we went over to their house. José exchanged a few words with a dark young man with curly hair and an angular face pitted with smallpox, whom the others called Viceroy. He talked with a thick Andalusian accent, and although he smiled, you could see from his eyes that he was tough. When we left, José told me that he was Jordi's wife's lover. 'A character you've got to be careful with,' he added. 'He'll take his knife out on the slightest provocation.'

Luciano and Miguel were waiting for us on the peak. Miguel had shot another pigeon and grazed a third, and he was drinking from Luciano's wineskin and looking happy.

'Here, come on,' he said. 'It's Sunday; we've got to get drunk.'

When my turn came, I lifted my elbow but the vinegary taste of the wine was unpleasant. Miguel seemed a little high, and suddenly he looked me right in the face.

'Well, what are you waiting for?' he said in a hoarse voice. 'Do you need women around to get drunk?'

I felt the blood rising to my cheeks, and I drank from the wineskin to hide it. José distributed the food. There were meat pies, roasted sausage, and tomatoes. With his mouth full, Luciano asked if now I would be coming to Mas more frequently. I said no, that this was good-bye, and when I looked up, I saw that Miguel's eyes were full of tears.

'Bah,' said José. Neither he nor Luciano had noticed. 'When you love a place, you can't leave it just like that. I bet you'll be coming every year.'

By lunch time we were back at Mas, and José showed our trophies. 'You have to congratulate Miguel,' he said. 'If someone challenged him to a gunfight, I'd bet on him.'

On the terrace, the wind had calmed down. Mara had just put the baby down for a nap and ran toward us. 'At last, my two darlings! . . . If you knew how alone I felt. . . . I had the feeling that I was a girl whose boyfriend had gone off to the war.' Lolita brought two bottles of claret, and we sat around the marble table. The record player was playing Bessie Smith singing *Saint Louis Blues*. While we drank, Luciano started on me and asked the others to witness that he'd make me promise to return in the fall.

'If you don't come to gather mushrooms, I swear I won't talk to you again.'

Mara said I wouldn't return unless some woman had finally won me.

'We'll have to find him some beautiful country girl,' she sighed.

'Isn't the country enough?' Luciano asked.

'Bruno is weak, and the French girls will catch him. Only love can save him.'

I had owed Régine a letter for three days, but my tiredness got the better of me, and after eating I slept until six without waking. Dora, Jorge, and Luis were drinking coffee in the gallery when I got up. Dora was dressed again in the style of the Twenties – ropes of pearls and short bangs – and she looked at me with her enormous, colorless eyes.

'We've just founded a Desperation Club,' she said. 'Do you want to join?'

I answered that I had never been so happy, but Jorge protested and insisted on explaining the rules of the game.

'We get drunk on coffee. This is our sixth cup. The first one who laughs loses.'

I was about to tell them that there were more important things to do, but I didn't, for some odd reason. In the garden a blackbird flapped around the top of the eucalyptus and finally perched on the top of the roof. Alvaro sat reading on the bench in the summer-house.

'They're crazy,' he said. 'Everyone in this house is crazy.' He said that Miguel was going through one of his moody phases and was locked up in his study.

'And Mara?' I asked.

'She went out with the baby to rake the woods. Miguel and she have had a spat. Didn't you hear?'

'No.'

'It was after coffee, while we were chatting. . . .'

'What about?'

'You ask him. I've given up trying to understand for a long time.'

I took his advice and went through the cork wood until I found her. Mara was gathering dead leaves in a basket while the baby played with acorns. When she saw me she looked at me coldly.

'Whom are you looking for?' she said.

I repeated my conversation with Alvaro and asked why she had fought with Miguel.

'Was it my fault?'

'Your fault?' Mara looked at me as if I were talking nonsense. 'On the contrary, he was just saying nice things about you. I think that you're one of the few persons he loves in his own way, if he really loves anyone. No, it wasn't because of you. It's Dora.'

Mara stopped raking and leaned on the trunk of a cork tree. 'I don't automatically take the woman's side, you know, and if you insist, I'll admit I'm also bothered by Dora's way of loving Armando. Dora is one of those women who don't let the man they love even breathe. But, my boy, that Miguelito is just too much sometimes.'

We walked toward the spring. Mara had the baby by the hand, and for a few minutes we were silent.

'Miguel is going through a bad time, and you should help him.'

'Do you think I help?' I said. 'I think he's been keeping an eye on me since the other afternoon. I feel him about to pounce on me, as if he were jealous of me.'

'Miguel is jealous of everybody,' she sighed. 'His relations with men are always morbid. That's why I'm always fighting with him. We've got to stop him from letting go.'

I told her about the scene that morning and added that I was thinking of leaving.

'You're crazy,' said Mara. 'You men can say things to each other that you'd never confess to a woman. You're not a child like the others. Miguel can confide in you. If you leave him, he's lost.'

'I've tried to talk to him a dozen times. I swear to you it's useless.'

'You men can understand each other without talking,' Mara argued. 'That's why I get along better with my men friends than I do with my women friends. I'd like to have a girl friend with whom I could talk the way we're talking now, but I've never found one. Women never stop talking about themselves. . . . With them, you can never be alone.'

It was getting dark as we went home. Mara had recovered her good humor, and the baby walked with her, absorbed in some secret monologue. The coffee jag had ended badly. Luis was recovering in his room, and Dora was taking tranquilizers. With his hair falling across his forehead, Jorge seemed even younger than his age. When he saw me, he grabbed my arm and dragged me out into the garden.

'I'm fed up,' he said. 'We're all leading a killing life. Don't think I talk nonsense for the hell of it. I'm just trying to be lucid. . . .'

'Drinking fifteen cups of coffee doesn't lead to anything,' I answered.

'Nothing leads to anything. Look at Miguel. He's worth more than any of us, but he undermines his own life. If we had his courage, we ought to do the same thing.'

I talked to him about Armando, but he obstinately shook his head. In fact, even he didn't take his own words seriously, and I slipped away and went to my own room to write Régine.

On Dora's visiting day, Miguel and Mara went out

after lunch in the Dauphine, and since it was also Midsummer Night's Eve, we made a date to meet at one of
the cafés on the Ramblas in Barcelona. Luis killed the
afternoon watching Lolita's comings and goings. During
the ride to the city, he announced solemnly that he
wanted to get drunk in order to forget. In Barcelona,
Alvaro phoned some friends from Geneva. The bonfires
gave the sky a reddish glow. The Plaza Real was jammed,
and we sat down at the Glaciar to have a drink.

The festival brought back a thousand memories. Under
the arcades, a compact crowd circulated – women with
paper hats, men in shirtsleeves, sweaty and lustful. Young
men ran by with trumpets, whistles, and rattles. Some of
them approached the girls and exploded firecrackers near
their legs. People seemed possessed by the noise. Firecrackers kept exploding without a stop, and even cars
looking for a parking spot honked their horns frantically.

Miguel was waiting for us at the Venezuela. We got
there half an hour late, and when I saw her swollen eyes,
I figured Dora had been crying. Mara said that Armando
was well and in good spirits; then she suddenly turned to
me and asked if I had phoned Gloria.

'Gloria?' I said. 'Why?'

'You men are really bastards. The poor girl is dying
for you, and it doesn't even occur to you to invite
her.'

I said that the others would intimidate her, but Mara
insisted and I had to give in.

Gloria was at home and said she would come right
away. 'Just long enough to get in a taxi. Ah, *tu es vraiment charmant.*'

Meanwhile, a group of Alvaro's friends had burst into
the bar : two Spanish girl students and a languid-looking
boy with dishevelled hair and astonished eyes. One of the

girls had dyed her hair jet black and painted her lips like
a little whore. The other one's make-up reminded one of
a mask, with a heavy covering of rice powder and lines of
black around the eyes.

'*Je m'appelle Alain,*' said the boy. '*Je suis né d'une
partouze et je suis le mineur le plus détourné de France.*'

The one with the mask for a face was called Luci, and
she told us that Alain and she had spent two weeks in the
Tyrol before coming to Barcelona. 'It's a sinister country,'
she said. 'People walk the street in narrow-waisted jackets
and conspirator's hats. Everyone gives the impression of
belonging to a secret society.'

The three talked and laughed very loudly and, following their example, Alvaro and Jorge also screamed.
Gloria showed up later in a kind of printed pajamas and
kissed me on the cheek. I introduced her to the others,
and Mara kissed her and said she had been anxious to
meet her.

'Bruno has spoken so much about you. . . . It's as if
we were friends already.'

It was impossible to keep a conversation going there,
and we went off through Escudillers among the balloon
sellers. The crowd covered the whole sidewalk, and to
make any progress we had to get out in the street. Dora
was crying again, so I took her arm. 'Come on,' I said.
'Don't be a child.' Wearing Cordoban hats they'd bought,
Luci and Alvaro were arguing ahead of us. I discovered
that Gloria and Mara were talking animatedly, and it
made me a little apprehensive.

Before reaching Aviño, we cut through a narrow side
street on the right, under a deluge of sparks. The eating
places smelled of fried food, and you could hear music
from jukeboxes and a band of gypsies clapping. Jorge
stuck his head into two or three bars. Finally we decided

on one which was decorated with immense barrels and had a very long bar covered with appetizers.

Alvaro ordered two pitchers of wine, and when we sat down, Mara put on a candid look and revealed that Gloria was writing a novel. 'A work of a psychological character,' she added.

There was a moment of silence, and I caught a malicious look from Miguel. 'In some ways it's an autobiography,' Gloria confided.

'May I ask for whom you're writing it?' asked Miguel.

'For whom I'm writing it?'

'When someone starts a novel, he has a public in mind,' explained Miguel. 'I'm asking what audience you're aiming it at.'

'I don't know,' murmured Gloria. 'I've never thought of that.'

'Then you're working in a vacuum? You're doing something without knowing why? How curious!'

'Well . . .' Gloria's look begged me to help her out. 'The fact is I write for myself.'

'For yourself?'

'Yes.'

'Then you write for the pleasure of reading yourself. . . .' Anger had revived Miguel. 'I guess it must be something very exciting.'

The arrival of the wine interrupted the conversation. Mara kept her innocent expression and gave Miguel a conspiratorial look. Gloria's execution seemed to have delighted her. Alvaro was talking in French with his friends. They were criticizing the wife of some Carlos or other who attempted suicide regularly with sleeping pills, and Dora broke in and said she knew some pills that never failed.

'You swallow a whole vial,' she said, 'and that's that.'

'Who are you talking about?' asked Luis.

'Alvaro says that suicides that don't come off are just farcical,' said Luci.

'I don't think so,' said Dora. 'Sometimes they can be sincere.'

The discussion went on for a few minutes – time enough to empty the two pitchers. Miguel was quiet, with the same somber despair as in his cavern the last few days.

'If you really want to make an end of everything, you go up to some tenth floor and fling yourself down instead of making a nuisance for others,' he said brusquely.

'I wouldn't be able to,' said Dora. 'It's a matter of esthetics.'

'Esthetics? What the hell does esthetics have to do with it? It's a question of being at peace forever, isn't it?'

'Yes, of course. Of course it is!' Dora spoke vehemently. 'But you have to think of others.'

'If you think of others, it means you still love life.'

Dora defended herself as if her own life were at stake, and for a moment I thought that Miguel was going to scream.

Mara intervened to calm them down. 'How about a change of air?' she suggested. 'I'm stifling here.'

We left, and in the street Dora cried quietly. 'I'm sincere, sincere. . . . I swear it – or may Armando suffer.'

The noisy festival crowd drowned out her words and Mara put her arm around Dora's waist. 'Pay no attention to him,' she said. 'He just talks for the sake of talking.'

'It's terrible. . . .' Dora watched the movement of the crowd fascinated. 'Everyone seems happy to be alive. Nobody knows what's happening. . . . They make you want to start screaming to wake them up.'

We stopped to drink at several bars, and Miguel would

order double gins and empty them in one gulp. Gloria
had recovered her aplomb and was laughing and flirting
with Alain. The jukebox music drowned out our voices.
At intervals we'd hear firecrackers exploding in the
street.

'Watch Miguel,' Mara whispered to me. 'Don't let him
do anything foolish.'

I was at the bar talking to Jorge, and I went over to
Miguel.

'Why don't we go to La Venta?' I said. 'We were there
the last time we saw each other, remember?'

'Bruno is a sentimentalist,' Miguel said to Jorge, but
his eyes stared at me ironically. 'His life reduces itself to a
collection of color postcards. Before he decided to dedicate
himself to women, he couldn't do enough for his friends.'

'What friends?' said Jorge.

'Armando, me, others. . . . In those days, the three of
us hoped to redeem humanity. Isn't that true, Bruno?'

'Yes,' I answered.

'Armando is the only one who's succeeded. Bruno and
I love humanity in general but we can't stand men. Time
has made us cynics.'

We were walking at a rapid pace toward La Venta, and
Miguel evoked those years of innocence and said that
women were at fault. 'You have to judge people by what
they do,' he murmured. 'Women drown us in psychology.'

The décor of the place hadn't changed. When we
entered, the girls at the bar were clapping and some
fellow was dancing the *gachucha*, wiggling his body and
gesticulating, as if his every movement obeyed some im-
perious logic, some absolutely ineluctable reason. At the
end of it the owner recognized me and came over to
embrace me. She was a plump blonde with large, freckled
forearms covered with bracelets.

'Well, it's Bruno,' she said. 'Where have you been, you rotten egg?'

I said that I had enrolled in the Foreign Legion at a recruiting post, and she accepted my explanation without blinking.

'Did you kill someone my boy?'

'Yes.'

'Hey, girls!' she yelled. 'A round of Moriles for my assassin.'

She herself got a sudden violent impulse to laugh, and it made her choke. One of the girls led us to the back room, and shortly after I sat down, I discovered that I was drunk. Gloria was talking shrilly in French, proud to be passing as a foreigner. A dancer flitted among the groups in a ruffled polka dot shirt. Dora looked around with sad eyes, and Mara pulled her toward her and they exchanged confidences in low voices.

'Eh you, Antonito!' yelled the owner. 'Dance a bit for the gentlemen.'

The young man delicately wiped away his perspiration. The guitarist tuned his instrument with one leg on a chair and began a fandango. The clients at the bar formed a circle around us. Next to the empty boxes at the back were a group of men dressed in working clothes, and Miguel called to them and invited them over to drink manzanilla.

'Thanks, pal,' said one blond. He smiled, showing his teeth, and raised his glass. 'To your health and that of your friends. To Catalonia!'

'Where are you from?' I asked.

'The three of us are Asturians, except for this one. He's from Galicia.'

The owner brought several bottles of Moriles, and the Asturians sat down at our table and looked excitedly at the women. The dancer twisted and turned for a long time amid the mocking applause of the audience. Miguel's guests were also getting tight, and one of them put his arm around my shoulder and said he worked at the piers as an extra hand.

'Those girls, are they friends of yours?'

'Yes.'

'How nice they are. Our wives are back home, you understand?'

The manzanilla went fast. Miguel never stopped filling our glasses, and the owner uncorked another two bottles. My neighbor whispered secrets in my ear, and I closed my eyes. When I opened them, Luis was snoring in a chair in the corner, and one of the Asturians was showing his biceps to Luci and insisting on taking his shirt off to show her his tattoos.

'Touch them,' he said. 'Don't be afraid.'

Later – for some unknown reason – Mara fought bitterly with Miguel. They exchanged insults in a half whisper, and I went out to the street to get some air.

'I'm fed up, Bruno. . . . I swear I can't take any more.' Mara had followed me, her eyes red with crying, and I took her in my arms. The ground gave under me. I pushed her against a door and flattened my lips against hers.

'No,' she said. 'No, no.'

She got loose with a sudden push and turned her back to me. The convulsive trembling of her shoulders told me she was crying again. 'I'm in love with Miguel,' she said in a muffled voice. 'I'd kill myself before I'd hurt him in the least.'

She had let her hands fall, and took out a handkerchief from her skirt. The neon sign from a movie house made her profile stand out clearly.

'Don't ruin everything, Bruno. . . . Promise me you won't do it again.'

A group of young fellows with paper hats and false noses ran by throwing firecrackers, and one of them blew a cardboard horn in my ear. The sky over the street was beginning to grow pale. Mara had suddenly disappeared, and I walked around the neighborhood until I was tired.

When I finally found her, she was in the Ramblas with the others. Gloria had gone in a Peugeot 403 with Alain's friends and the Asturians, and she yelled from the car window that they were going to see the dawn from the breakwater.

'We'll wait for you there,' she said.

The return trip to Mas was very long. Jorge drove making S's, and Miguel smoked, pale and with circles under his eyes. Mara drove the Dauphine with the others. At every crossing the dawn threw a pale light on the vestiges of the festival. People were still out wearing paper hats, but the bars were closing one by one; in the main street of the town we heard bells ringing and saw several groups of women walking hurriedly to church.

Hours later – as if by an electric contagion – a quarrel broke out again between the two tenant families. Still half asleep, I heard lamentations and insults, and when I got up to open the shutters, Damiana and Lolita's older sister were screaming at each other in the middle of the vegetable garden, and threatening to come to blows. Their families lined up behind each of them, as if weighing their respective forces. The children took in the scene, tiny and wide-eyed. The dogs barked excitedly. His arms crossed over his chest, José looked sad and beaten.

Jorge was showering in the bathroom and told me that they had been going on this way for three hours. The reason for the row was apparently hard to figure out. Some mocking grimace at the wash house, according to some ; a push by Damiana, according to others. 'Damiana and the old woman urged the men on,' he said. 'Miguel had to go down to calm them down.'

My head ached from the hangover, and I went up to the clearing to sunbathe. There wasn't the slightest breeze that morning. The sawing noise of the cicadas mingled with the buzzing of the bees in the madrone trees, and I dived in the pond several times and spent a long time floating.

Dora and Jorge came up to bathe before lunch. When I went back to the terrace, I met José on the path. He was barefoot and had his pants rolled up to his knees. When he saw me he smiled and made a vague gesture.

'Did you hear the screaming ?' he asked.

I said yes; he lit the butt hanging from his lips and said that the women were always pulling and pushing and arching their backs about some nonsense.

'I wish I knew where they keep their brains,' he said. 'I'm sure it's not in their heads.'

Alvaro and Miguel were drinking Perelada in the gallery. Mara was listening to Marlene's record, and she told me that I had a letter from Régine.

'My boy, I don't know what you give your women. They can't seem to live without you.'

While she looked through the record covers, she steered the conversation around to Gloria. She had obviously been thinking about her in my absence, and she said that she was very good-looking. 'She's a splendid type, don't you agree?'

There was a silence. Miguel drummed on the table with his fingers, and Alvaro said he didn't like her.

'No?' said Mara. 'Why not?'

'I don't know. It has something to do with her skin. She doesn't do anything for me.'

'Naturally, I don't have the same basis for an opinion, but if she interests a tomcat like Bruno, I imagine she must have something.' Mara smiled maliciously and explained that Gloria was the kind of girl who dreams of marrying a prince.

'Let's admit it could happen,' she added. 'You like her.'

'Bruno likes any woman,' said Miguel. 'He'd fall in love with a scarecrow if it wore a skirt.'

Régine wrote that her father was well now, and asked me to return to Paris Thursday. Her energy worked the miracle of shaking me out of my torpor. I sent a telegram to Blaye immediately and telephoned the offices of Iberia to reserve a seat on the morning plane.

After lunch, Miguel and Mara shut themselves up in their room, and I slept the afternoon through without waking. My throat was dry when I got up, and my head throbbed. The record player was playing by itself in the gallery. Dora was walking in the garden with a melancholy air.

'Shall we take a walk?' she suggested.

I walked with her under the cork trees, and we talked about Brecht's and Stanislavsky's theories. The knowledge that forty-eight hours later I would be living far from there saddened me profoundly. Above the summit of Montnegre there was a band of pink clouds. The sun had not yet completely set behind the mountain, but there was a light breeze and its coolness was pleasant.

When we got back to Mas, the sunlight cut across the French windows of the gallery. Alain and his friends had landed with a dozen visitors. The record player was playing Goyita, and two girls in shirts and jeans were dancing the charleston.

From the footbridge I heard a girl cry, 'Look, she's
drinking cognac the way old men do. . . . It's out of
fashion,' and a chorus of voices insisted, 'Out, out!'
Miguel and Mara had lain down on the divan, and
Miguel talked in that feverish, voluble manner he affec-
ted in public when he wanted to be charming or when he
was getting drunk.

'I've been trying to explain for a long time that their
class enemy is me and that they should unite against me,
but it's no use. They all find me enchanting.'

'That's true,' said Mara. She leaned over and kissed
him impulsively on the lips. 'You're the most enchanting
person in the world.'

For a while I drifted from group to group. Jorge had
opened a bottle of gin, and I helped Dora make cuba
libres. At one end of the gallery some older man was
talking about a certain Juan Carlos who had hit a child
with his car and whom the victim's family was suing for
half a million pesetas. 'And what do you think he answered?' he said. 'Impossible! For that price every
mother in Spain would start flinging children in front of
cars.' There was a chorus of exclamations, and I went
over to Alain. Luis was dancing with the student with
dyed hair we'd met the night before. Luci had sat down
on a cushion on the floor and was telling Alvaro how the
festival had ended.

'Your Asturians turned out to be regular brutes.
Imagine, when they got in the car they wanted to take us
to some lonely spot.'

'Alain agreed,' said the other. 'The dirty traitor.'

'Luci and Nuria are terrible snobs. To rape them
you've got to have read Robbe-Grillet.'

'The one next to me kept pinching me. He'd say: "If
you come with me you'll never forget it."'

'Maybe it was true,' said Alain. 'In such cases, one gives it a try.'

'Why didn't you then, my boy?'

'Because no one propositioned *me*. Do you think I would've let such a chance go by?'

'Look at my arm, it's still full of bruises.'

'The one with the tattoos tried to kiss me,' said Nuria.

'You egged him on first,' said Alain in a falsetto voice. 'I saw it in the rear-view mirror.'

The girls protested, and I asked what had happened to Gloria.

'We don't know.' Luci made a helpless gesture. 'I remember absolutely nothing.'

Marlene Dietrich was singing the foxtrot from *The Blue Angel*. Mara took off her shoes to dance, and I did a few turns with her.

'I invited them to surprise Miguel,' she said. 'Poor fellow, he needs to see people. Intellectual work depresses him.'

It was our first private chat since I had kissed her on the street, and I said I was sorry about what had happened.

'You men are children,' she sighed. 'Miguel, you, Jorge. ... You bore me, I swear.' Mara leaned her forehead on my cheek and her voice changed. 'On Sunday we're going to Tossa. The German women are mad about the fishermen. Jorge says it has a lot of atmosphere. . . .'

When I told her I couldn't go, she pulled her head back a few inches to look at me. 'No?'

'I'm leaving the day after tomorrow. Régine is waiting for me in Paris. I've got a reservation.'

'I thought you were joking. . . .' Her surprise seemed genuine.

'No, Mara, I can't stay any longer.'

'You're hateful. Just when I was beginning to get along well with you, you're taking off. Miguel will be furious.'

When the record was over, I sat down on the floor with the others. The conversation had left a bitter taste in my mouth. Lolita was going from one to the other filling glasses, and I noticed that Luis followed her to the kitchen. 'It's now or never,' Alvaro confided to me. 'Let's see what happens.' On my right, a blonde about thirty years old complained about the close watch her husband kept on her. 'To deceive him I have to pick up our son at school. Instead of going by trolley, I take a taxi, and Paco and I can then spend exactly twenty minutes together, between six twenty-five and a quarter to seven. I have to lie to my maid, the doorman, the landlord. It's terribly complicated, I assure you. I swear, I'll end up being faithful out of laziness!' Nuria gave a laugh. 'Twenty minutes is enough for you?' she exclaimed. Alain laughed too, and told a story about a writer in Geneva who had two girl friends, one blonde and one dark, and justified his inability to turn out any work by saying that the only time he had to himself he spent sweeping the blond hairs off the floor when he was expecting the dark one and the black hairs when he expected the blonde. 'Why don't you find him a redhead besides?' said Luci. Their nonsense bored me, and I went out to the garden.

The moon floated like a balloon above the eucalyptuses. The frogs croaked in the pond, and I could make out some shadows in the summer house. As I drew closer, I recognized Miguel and Jorge with several young men I didn't know. A baritone voice assured everyone that the Mediterranean didn't make him feel one way or the other. 'I'm from Meseta, the land of poplars. I don't understand olives.' Another answered that he preferred the light in Ibiza, and I decided the two of them must be painters.

Little by little the others came to join us. Mara and the women had taken over the divans in the gallery and laughed excitedly. 'They're having fun at our expense,' said Luis. 'I wanted to butt in and they threw me out.'

'Let's do the same,' said Alvaro. 'Let's criticize them.'

His proposition fell on deaf ears, and, for an interminable time, the painters discussed the respective merits of the circle and the cube. The one from Meseta praised the simple structure and the voluptuousness of angles; his companion, the generous, profoundly maternal form of the sphere. Miguel was quiet, sober, and taciturn, on the verge of one of his explosions of anger. On the other side of the valley little lights went on and off at intervals, and suddenly Miguel turned to me and pointed to them.

'That must be Luciano and his family,' he murmured. 'They're looking for snails.'

'Why don't we go with them?'

Miguel shook his head. The moonlight delicately lit his features, and a nostalgia for our beautiful lost friendship overwhelmed me.

'You're right,' he said. 'Snails at least are real. If they don't eat them, they can sell them in town. Here, we're trying to chase ghosts.'

We had understood each other without the need for words, and when we reached the footbridge, he smiled sadly and wished me good night.

With mourning in my heart, I walked in the garden outside the gallery, hoping to have a really frank talk with Mara, but Alain's friends made it impossible. When the gin was gone, Jorge invented some devilish mixture, and at midnight the whole party went up to bathe in the pond. From the terrace I could hear them splashing and yelling, and I decided to follow Miguel's example. When I turned out the light, I opened the door to the corridor. I was sure that Mara would come, and I didn't fall asleep until very late.

The last day a strange fever ran all through Mas. Doors opened and closed violently, and, still half asleep, I heard Dora's high-pitched voice and the sound of hurrying footsteps. I made an effort and got up to see what was happening. Damiana was sobbing in the kitchen and told me that Armando was out of jail.

Jorge and the women had gone to get him in the Dauphine, and I went up to the cavern to embrace Miguel. Bright tears ran down his face uncontrollably. He had the orphaned expression he'd had as a child, and with an acuteness that surprised me, I took the measure of our helplessness – Miguel's and mine and Mara's – in the face of life's cruelties.

'Well,' he said. 'We'll have to find some other excuse.' Miguel spoke very calmly and slowly lit a cigarette. 'For the moment, the party's over.'

DATE DUE